HARD PASS

A ST. LOUIS MAVERICKS HOCKEY ROMANCE

BRENDA ROTHERT

KAT MIZERA

SILVER SKY PUBLISHING, INC.

CHAPTER ONE

Sariah

I WAS NEVER GETTING another pet.

No way, no how.

Losing them hurt too damn much.

I let myself into my apartment and sighed, realizing that Mr. Pebbles would never again come running to greet me, rubbing up on my legs and letting me know he missed me.

Today had been hard. Harder than finding my fiancé in bed with another woman, harder than having to tell my family that our wedding was off, and even harder than having to get a second job to pay the rent for our apartment after he moved out.

None of that had prepared me for putting my sweet cat to sleep.

My phone rang and I dug it out of my purse, holding it between my ear and shoulder as I answered. "Hey, Dee."

"How are you?" My best friend's voice was filled with sympathy.

"Awful," I said, putting my purse down and padding into the master bedroom. "I may have cried more today than I did when I found out Theo was cheating."

"Want me to come over? We could get takeout and watch *Jaws* or something," she said, knowing that was one of my favorite movies.

"I think I'm going to soak in the tub and go to bed early," I said. "I'm working a double tomorrow at the restaurant, so I need to rest."

"Can you take a few days off?" she asked. "Jobs pay for bereavement leave for the death of a spouse, and a cat is way harder to lose than a husband. In my jaded opinion, anyway."

"I don't have any paid time off, and I need the money, especially after today. And anyway, sitting home moping will just make me feel worse. When I'm at the restaurant, I'm too busy to think, which is exactly what I need."

"It would be way more fun if we went out and got stupid drunk, danced on a bar somewhere, and then you fell into bed with some rando."

I laughed. Dee, whose full name was Desiree, thought all problems could be solved with a night out.

"Last time I let you talk me into that, I wound up hooking up with Theo. Three years later, look where I am."

"It's not my fault you turned your nose up at the very hot rocker dude who was into you. Instead, you went for the clean-cut accountant."

"Tell me about it," I muttered.

"You sure you don't want me to come over?"

"Not tonight. I really just want to chill and get to sleep early."

"Okay. Call me tomorrow on your break and let me know how you're doing."

"Thanks, hon. Talk to you later." I disconnected and went into the bathroom. A bath sounded like a great idea, and since I couldn't afford this place on my own, I was going to enjoy the massive bathtub as much as possible before I moved.

I poured a glass of wine while the tub was filling and then stripped off my clothes. I poured a few drops of essential oil into the tub and stepped into the hot water, easing down happily. Tension drained out of me and I leaned back.

I'd been looking for a smaller, more affordable apartment since Theo had moved out, but there was no way to break our lease early, and I had two months left on it. I had several good prospects when the time came, but none of them had deep soaker tubs like this one. Or gourmet kitchens and walk-in closets the size of some people's bedrooms.

Ugh. Moving was going to suck.

I closed my eyes, refusing to dwell on all of that. Theo was gone and I never had to think about, talk to, or see him ever again.

Oh, shit.

I opened my eyes and frowned.

Mr. Pebbles had been *our* cat, though I'd refused to give him up when Theo moved out. Now that I'd had to put him down, it seemed like I should at least tell Theo what happened. I loathed the idea of reaching out to my ex, but it felt like the right thing to do. The mature, responsible, adult thing to do.

Ha.

That was funny since Theo had said I was imma-ture and unsophisticated.

As if having threesomes made you sophisticated.

I stared at my phone, trying to remember the number.

Was it bad that I'd dated Theo for two years and couldn't remember his phone number?

I'd deleted every single reminder of him, from his contact information to all our pictures. But now I needed his phone number if I was going to text him. It had a lot of sevens, that much I knew.

Was it 776-0771?

Or was it 0773?

Shit.

I racked my brain, trying to remember the last time I'd dialed his number, but it had been saved as a favorite before I deleted it, so I hadn't had to after the very first time. Squinting a little, as if that would help, I typed in the first phone number that had come to mind. It felt like the right combination and I typed out my message quickly, hoping to get this over with.

SARIAH: I just wanted to let you know Mr. Pebbles passed away today. I had to have him put down.

I wasn't sure if he would answer. We hadn't ended on the best of terms, obviously, but Mr. Pebbles had been his cat too. He couldn't be that coldhearted, could he?

To my surprise, he responded right away.

THEO: Sorry to hear that.

Sorry to hear that?!

That was all he'd been able to come up with? He

really was a heartless bastard. I got pissed off all over again. It wasn't his fault that Mr. Pebbles had died, but couldn't he at least show a little sympathy?

SARIAH: That's it? That's all you have to say?

THEO: Well, I'm not sure what this is about, so...

SARIAH: I just told you! Mr. Pebbles is dead.

THEO: How did I know him?

SARIAH: Are you high right now? He was our cat. Black and white, took a shit in your shoes more than once? Ringing any bells?

THEO: I think you have the wrong number. But I'm really sorry about your cat. I lost one when I was a teenager and it was hard.

Oh, hell.

Did I really have the wrong number or was Theo fucking with me? That was exactly the kind of thing he would do to avoid a confrontation.

SARIAH: Is this really the wrong number? You're not Theo?

THEO: Nope.

SARIAH: I apologize. I deleted all of my ex's contact info when we broke up and I was guessing on the number. Shit. I'm sorry I bothered you.

TEXT LABEL TBD: It's okay. I'm truly sorry about your cat, though. It's never easy to put down a pet.

SARIAH: I was thinking that today, I don't think I

want to ever go through this again. It's been horrible. Heartbreaking. Expensive. Zero stars. Do not recommend.

TEXT LABEL TBD: Yeah, I think I gave it one star myself. And the one star was for all the years of fun I had with her before she died.

I set my phone on the ledge of the tub. Was this getting weird? I was having a full conversation with someone I didn't even know. I pictured Mr. Pebbles curled up on my bed purring and burst into tears for the thirty-eighth time today. Then I took a giant gulp from my wineglass and picked up my phone again. Yes, it was getting weird. But I was sad, dammit, and this person seemed nice. Bonus, it was *not* Theo.

SARIAH: That's one of the worst things about this— she was only three. My ex and I found a litter of kittens on the street when we first met. We found homes for all of them except her. We kept her. And named her Pebbles. Until we went to get her fixed and found out she was a he. Hence, Mr. Pebbles.

TEXT LABEL TBD: He was only three?

SARIAH: Yup. Cancer sucks.

TEXT LABEL TBD: I'm sorry. I hope you're doing something nice for yourself tonight.

SARIAH: I'm actually soaking in the tub right now. I wanted to text Theo and get it over with, but apparently my objective this evening is to bore a stranger with my sad tale of euthanasia and horrible exes.

TEXT LABEL TBD: LOL that's okay. I'm having a quiet evening myself. I'm on a business trip and sitting here in my hotel room channel surfing. My coworkers are down at the bar getting shit-faced but I did that last night, so tonight I'm being good because I can't be hungover tomorrow.

SARIAH: My best friend suggested we go out and get shit-faced but I wasn't in the mood. And this is how I wound up in the tub texting with a stranger. My mother would be horrified.

TEXT LABEL TBD: On a scale of one to ten for all things dangerous and immoral, this is probably a one. Maybe a two if you're married.

SARIAH: A five if you're married too.

TEXT LABEL TBD: How come you only got one extra point for being married but I got three points on top of that???

SARIAH: Maybe because 1 + 0 = 1 but 1 + 1 = 5?

TEXT LABEL TBD: ROFL! Well, you're in luck. I am one-thousand-percent single. Not even dating.

SARIAH: That makes two of us, so I guess we're back down to a one on our scale of dangerous and immoral.

TEXT LABEL TBD: And as a bonus, we don't have to do any of that complicated math stuff. Good thing. Math is not my favorite.

SARIAH: I like numbers. But I'm in sales so I kind of have to. There's no advanced math like calculus or any of that in my life, though. Addition, subtraction, multiplication, and division are as complicated as it gets.

TXT LABEL TBD: I think I failed Algebra in high school.

SARIAH: I needed a tutor.

TEXT LABEL TBD: Okay, so zero stars for math too.

SARIAH: And ex-boyfriends who cheat.

TEXT LABEL TBD: And ex-girlfriends who cheat.

SARIAH: Touché.

TEXT LABEL TBD: However, I'll give five stars to unexpected text conversations with strangers who hate math.

SARIAH: LOL agreed. Thank you for being so nice tonight. You really didn't have to spend half an hour texting with a stranger.

TEXT LABEL: If you tell me your name, we won't be strangers anymore.

Was it dumb to tell him my name? Probably not. I could just block him once we finished talking.

SARIAH: I'm Sariah. Nice to meet you.

TEXT LABEL TBD: That's a pretty name. I'm Rob :)

SARIAH: Thank you. Anyway, I really appreciate you. I needed someone to talk to tonight and you made me smile. But I've taken up enough of your time. Also, my bathwater is cold.

ROB: No problem at all. If you feel like talking again, hit me up. I'm on the road until next week, so I'm usually in my hotel room staring at the TV when I'm not working or in meetings.

For the first time since we'd started talking, I felt a moment of unease. It had been fun to chat with someone who knew nothing about me, but kind of weird in a way too. He seemed nice enough, but was probably a forty-year-old porn addict who lived in his mom's basement. And the last thing I needed was some weird internet stalker.

SARIAH: I have a long day tomorrow and there's a lot going on because I have an important interview next week. I'm not sure what my schedule will be going forward.

ROB: No worries. Drop a text if you feel like it. If not, take care.

SARIAH: You too.

I put the phone down and took another long drink of wine. Part of me was still wondering if it was actually Theo fucking with me, but he wouldn't have been that nice. Or that patient. Then again, to get out of paying for half the vet bill, I wouldn't put anything past him.

I was probably too suspicious for my own good, but I'd sworn off all men. Even sweet, faceless mystery men I only knew via text. Whoever he was, Rob had been a good distraction on a day when I desperately needed one. But that was that.

Peace out, Rob. Have a nice life.

CHAPTER TWO

Nash

"I saw your picture on the El train the other day when I went to Chicago," my teammate Boone said, shaking his head. "It's so fucking weird seeing your goofy mug doing that smolder thing in a little Speedo."

I laughed. "I wasn't smoldering, and it wasn't a Speedo. But if it makes you feel less butt hurt about not being chosen as one of the sexiest athletes alive, keep 'em coming."

He gave me an exasperated look. "Dude, I was happy for you. But your damn picture is *everywhere*. On the magazine at my doctor's office, on billboards…enough already."

We were in the locker room after hockey practice, making small talk after showering.

As I put on a clean T-shirt, I said, "The world needs to know about the sexiness, man. It's out of my control."

It had been months since the magazine spread featuring me as one of the 15 Sexiest Athletes Alive had come out. And to be honest, I was pretty sick of all the attention myself. But when you're a hockey player, teammates will seize any opportunity to chirp at you. For a month after the article and photos came out, I'd walked into the locker room to see a different photoshopped variation of one of the photos every day. A rookie named Eric Alvarado had started it, and his favorite one was a photo of me standing on a beach that he'd added long, flowing Fabio hair to. Rookies with big enough balls to do that to a veteran had to be put in their place. And I wasn't about to let Alvarado know he'd gotten on my nerves—that wasn't my style.

Our team captain, Wes, walked over and gave me a wry look. "Hey, I've got a fantastic opportunity for you, man."

"Let me guess. Babysitting?"

"Well, since you're offering." He grinned. "Lars always has plans now that he's with Sheridan. And Annalise loves it when you bring your dog."

"*Dogs*. I have three, dude, and Athena and Louie get their feelings hurt when Archie gets to go somewhere and they don't. Last time Athena gave me sad eyes for a full twenty-four hours afterward."

"Hell, bring 'em all," Wes said. "The kids love the bulldog, but they'll play with all of them. Hadley and I are desperate for a night out since I'll actually be home this weekend, and our usual sitter has plans."

"Yeah, I'll do it. For pizza."

My teammate gave me a grateful look. "Any pizza you want, man. As many as you want. Thank you."

"Who the fuck put this on my car?"

Wes and I looked over to see Eric Alvarado, who had just stormed into the locker room with a magnetic bumper sticker in hand. He could be a hothead and we all knew it, so everyone mostly ignored him. I didn't even look his way.

Then the snickering started. My teammates were reading the bumper sticker. I smiled.

I didn't have to look at it to know what it said. Ask Me About my Micropenis. I'd snuck it onto the bumper of his truck when we got home from our road trip yesterday, knowing he wouldn't see it since he always backed into his parking space.

"I know it was you, Reilly," he said, coming over to me and slamming it down on the wooden bench I stood next to. "You think you're so funny."

"I have no idea what you're talking about," I said, keeping my expression neutral. "But I do have some questions about your micropeen."

Someone on the other side of the locker room laughed out loud, and a vein in Alvarado's forehead started throbbing.

"Dude, Laura and I are living with her parents while our house is being remodeled, and her dad's a pastor," Eric said. "My father-in-law wasn't amused when he saw this on my truck in his driveway."

Wes approached Eric, stopping right next to him and crossing his arms.

"You seem to be able to dish it out but not take it," he said.

Eric rolled his eyes. "Those pictures of Nash were all in good fun. They didn't hurt anyone."

Wes furrowed his brow, confused. "If that bumper sticker hurt someone, they need to nut up."

"Hey, I've got somewhere I need to be," I said, picking up the magnetic bumper sticker and sliding it into my bag. "See you guys tomorrow."

"We're not done here, Nash," Alvarado said.

I scoffed. "Yeah, we are. I wouldn't say another word if I were you, but you're not the smartest guy, so do you have anything else to say?"

Wes clapped him on the shoulder. "Nope, he's good. Right, Eric?"

I didn't look back to see if Alvarado would say anything else. I knew he wouldn't. No one fucked with their team captain. At least no one who wanted to stay on a team. And Eric wasn't exactly in demand, so he'd keep his mouth shut.

I grinned. That had gone well. And he'd even given me the bumper magnet back, so I could put it back on his truck after the next road trip.

———

WHEN I WALKED into my house after practice, the welcoming committee descended on me, tails wagging.

Louie, my black bernedoodle, was the biggest, so I wasn't even able to set down my keys and bag before his feet were on my chest and he was giving me a kiss. Athena, my German shepherd mix, had been taught manners by a previous owner before I got her from the local rescue all three of my dogs came from, so she hung back, sitting and waiting. Her tail still swished, though. And my bulldog Archie waited for me to bend down and greet him like I always did. He was seven now, and his jumping days were over.

"Were you guys good?" I asked them. "Do you want to eat?"

That always got them excited—especially Archie. I went into my laundry room and opened the closet full of dog supplies, scooping every dog's individual food into their bowls.

They cost me a ton of money, but my dogs were my family. All three of them had been rescued from bad situations, and I employed a local guy who fed and cared for them when I couldn't because of my hockey schedule. When I went on road trips, he stayed at my house to dog sit.

While the dogs ate, I checked my phone, wondering if Sariah had texted. Something about her had intrigued me when we exchanged texts the day before yesterday. I liked that she seemed to be putting her thoughts directly out there, telling me what she was really thinking and feeling.

A downside of being me was that women usually tried to be impressive. They always seemed to be "on" with full faces of makeup, filtered photos, and an eagerness to do whatever I wanted to do. Tinder was loaded with women looking for a partner to "adventure" with, complete with mountain climbing and sailing photos.

What I missed about having someone was the completely unscripted moments. Cooking brunch together, no one caring how their hair looked in the morning, or what shoes they had on.

The at-home weekend look was one of my biggest turn-ons—a woman wearing a pair of boxers and a tank top, with no makeup on and her long hair piled on top of her head in a messy bun. Even better if she was wearing glasses.

As a pro hockey player who'd been named one of the fifteen sexiest athletes, I hadn't seen that side of a woman in a long time. I guess that was why I'd told Sariah my name was Rob—just in case she connected the name Nash with the sexiest athlete thing.

No messages from her. And damned if that wasn't refreshing in itself. She was single, obviously —she'd told me about her breakup. So reaching out to her wouldn't be wrong.

I typed out a message.

NASH: Hi Sariah. Hope things are going better for you.

Archie, always the first dog to finish his food, came waddling into the kitchen and I set my phone down on the counter.

"Hey bud, you want to go outside?"

I'd had a doggie door installed last summer—best decision ever—but I was still in the habit of asking the dogs if they wanted to go out after they ate. Archie waited until I'd scratched all his favorite places, and then he headed for the doggie door.

I made myself a sandwich and grabbed a bag of chips from the pantry, and when I sat down at the table to eat, I saw that Sariah had responded.

SARIAH: Are you really a man?

I lowered my brows, amused, taking a giant bite of my sandwich before responding.

NASH: Just checked my pants and found a sausage and two meatballs, so yep, I can confirm that I'm a man.

SARIAH: I'm feeling stabby toward your sex right now. I'm a waitress, and a huge table of guys in suits came into the place I work for lunch. Two-hour lunch. All of them had top-shelf drinks. They tipped nine percent.

NASH: WTF? Not all men are assholes. I always tip at least twenty-five percent.

SARIAH: It seems like the people who have the least to give are always the most generous tippers.

NASH: My dad always said if you need a volunteer, ask a busy person, and if you need some money, ask a poor person.

SARIAH: It shouldn't be that way, but it is. Rich people are selfish. It's gross.

NASH: Did you ever reach Theo about the cat?

SARIAH: No. Fuck him. NEW SUBJECT. Is your day going better than mine?

Archie came back into the kitchen from the doggie door, his nails clacking on the hardwood floors. The other two had gone out there after him.

He flopped down onto the floor by my feet and I took a photo of him before sending it to Sariah.

NASH: This is my guy Archie. Hard to have a bad day with him around. He's one of three.

SARIAH: Rob, he's beautiful! I just want to smoosh his face and snuggle him. You have three dogs!?

Why had I told her my name was Rob? She hadn't even asked. We could have remained two anonymous people, getting to know someone we'd never meet in real life.

NASH: Couldn't help myself. They're family, you know? Do you think you'll get another pet? Not soon, but someday?

SARIAH: I don't know. My head says no but if I take one step into an animal shelter, my heart will drop-kick my head and I'll walk out of there with something warm and furry.

I smiled at her answer.

NASH: Pets are the best. They'd never tip you nine percent, and they'd fight anyone else who did.

SARIAH: With Mr. Pebbles, it would have depended on the day. He had so much attitude. A complete sense of entitlement. If I gave him the canned food with chunks of beef instead of salmon, he'd give me a murderous look. I miss that asshole.

NASH: It sounds like you gave him a good life.

SARIAH: Thanks. I hope I did. But it definitely wasn't long enough. I have to put my phone away and get back to work. Shitty tippers be wanting their food.

NASH: Hope the tips get better.

SARIAH: Thanks. Give Archie a smooch for me.

CHAPTER THREE

Sariah

I smoothed my hands down my dress pants and took a deep breath before stepping inside the Warren Center. I was smart, professional, and experienced, but job interviews made me nervous. Especially one like this. I'd never dreamed I'd get called for an interview when I'd impulsively sent in my résumé to the sales department of the local professional hockey team, the St. Louis Mavericks. They'd called and done a phone interview first, and now they wanted to meet me. It was as unnerving as it was exciting.

Originally, I hadn't thought much of it. I liked my job as a sales rep for a local weekly newspaper called the *Weekly Grind*. The problem was that I made a small base salary and everything else was commission. The paper wasn't doing well at the moment, so it was getting more and more difficult to get local businesses to advertise, which impacted my commissions. Some of my regulars had admitted to me in confidence that they just weren't seeing a return anymore. I'd had to start waiting tables part time to make ends meet after Theo left six months ago, because the paper had eliminated bonuses.

Everything would be easier once I moved out of my ridiculously expensive apartment. It would be even better if I got this job working for the Mavericks. I didn't know much about hockey, but I'd done my research the last week, watching every game I could find online and learning about both the team and the sport.

I walked into the arena and a tall, middle-aged man approached me with a smile. "Sariah? I'm Lance Becker, head of sales and marketing."

"Hello. Nice to meet you." I was surprised that the head of sales would be here to greet me personally.

"My secretary's kids all have strep, so I told her to stay home." He chuckled. "So I'll be showing you around myself."

"Well, I appreciate it."

"I thought we'd take a brief tour of the Warren Center while we get to know each other, and then we can sit down with a few members of the sales team when we get upstairs."

"Sounds perfect." I fell into step beside him as we walked toward a bank of elevators.

"Are you a hockey fan?" he asked as we stepped inside.

"I'm learning to be," I admitted. I'd been prepared for this question. I couldn't outright lie, because I'd undoubtedly fail if he tested me, but I thought I had a good response. "I was raised by family big on soccer so hockey wasn't really a thing for me until I got to college. I enjoyed going to live games, but to be honest, tickets to Mavericks games haven't been in the budget. I did go to one a couple of weeks ago though and it was amazing."

"If you enjoy live hockey, I think this job may be a good fit since you'll be here for most of the home games.

We stepped off the elevator and turned a corner. "This floor is where the private boxes are," he said. "If we extend you the job offer, you'll probably spend a good deal of time here making sure your clients are happy and having a good time."

"These are beautiful," I said, taking in the spacious box we'd just entered. The chairs were upholstered and expensive looking, with a huge TV on one wall, a bar in the corner, and best of all, the most amazing view of the ice.

"I don't think I'd have much trouble selling box seats," I said, thinking about a few of my wealthier clients from the newspaper. I'd made those connections on my own and I'd use every tool in my arsenal to be successful if I got this job.

"That's good to hear."

He showed me the press box, the locker room, some of the more expensive seats in the arena, and finally, the executive offices, which were on the top floor. Like everything else, they hadn't spared any expense here and even the cubicles out on the sales floor were high end and impressive. Hell, the break room was almost as nice as my kitchen at home.

As we walked down a hallway toward a conference room, I noticed a huge poster of an underwear ad. I paused, peering up at it curiously. The guy in the photo was drop-dead gorgeous, with the kind of body that probably made women all over the world lose their minds, and eyes so blue I was momentarily mesmerized. How could anyone be that hot? It had to be photoshopped, right?

"That's Nash Reilly," Mr. Becker told me, following my gaze. "He's one of our star forwards."

"I've read about him," I said, still looking at the ad. "But what's the underwear ad about?"

"The company approached him about doing a campaign for them, and since it doesn't interfere with hockey, he did it. It's given the team a bit of notoriety as well, so it's been win-win."

"I can imagine."

I could also imagine this guy being an arrogant prick.

Exactly the kind of guy I avoided in my life.

Well, I probably wouldn't have a lot of contact with the players anyway, but I could potentially use this type of popularity to my advantage when it came to selling ticket packages. I made a mental note to write that down as soon as I had a chance.

"Here we are." Lance let me walk into the conference room ahead of him and several men I assumed were from the sales team all turned to me. They ran the gamut from late twenties to middle age, and I tried to visualize myself among them. They looked friendly enough, which was encouraging, so I hoped my lack of in-depth hockey knowledge wouldn't hurt me. The compensation package was five times better than anything I had now, and the potential for bonuses was almost unlimited. I'd have to bust my ass to learn everything there was to know about selling season tickets to hockey games, but I was confident I could do a great job here.

Now all I had to do was convince them to hire me.

———

I'D FIGURED the interview would last an hour, maybe two, but I was there for almost four hours. By the time I left, I'd had to speed home, change clothes, and then turn around and head right back out for my shift at the restaurant. I'd had to close tonight, so I didn't get home until after midnight and it was the first time I could relax all day. I thought about running a bath, but I was too tired even for that and I threw myself facedown across the bed.

I was trying to decide whether I wanted a shower and a snack, just a snack, or to just turn off the lights and go to sleep when I heard my phone buzzing, indicating someone was texting me. Assuming it was Dee, wanting to know how the interview went, I turned over and grabbed it.

To my surprise, there was a text from Rob.

ROB: Hey, how'd the interview go?

He'd remembered.

I didn't really even know the guy and he'd remembered I had an interview today.

SARIAH: I think it went well.

ROB: Are you going to tell me what kind of job it is?

SARIAH: Not until I find out if I got it. I don't want to jinx it.

ROB: LOL fair enough. Did you work your other job tonight?

SARIAH: I did. I'm so tired I don't even have the energy to get something to eat. And my feet are killing me.

ROB: I give a great foot massage.

SARIAH: Oh, man, don't tease me. I'd kill for one right now.

Part of me wasn't sure if I should go down this route with him, but other than my phone number and first name, he didn't know anything about me, so I felt pretty safe as far as flirting was concerned.

ROB: Kind of hard to do the massage thing via text, but you should definitely treat yourself if you get the job.

SARIAH: No massages in my future until I move out of this apartment. My ex and I were sharing the rent, and he left me high and dry with the lease when he moved out. That's why I had to get a second job.

ROB: What a shithead. I'm sorry he did that to you. Your landlord wouldn't let you out of the lease because of extenuating circumstances?

SARIAH: No. He's a shithead too. But I've found an apartment in my friend Dee's building. It's in a nice, safe area and has underground parking and a pool. It's also a gated community, so that's perfect for a single woman living alone.

ROB: For sure. How long until you can move?

SARIAH: Two long months. Assuming I get offered this new job, I have to remember to mention that I'll need a few days off to move.

ROB: You got this. I can feel it.

I smiled to myself. Even if he was some loser living with his mom, he was a nice loser.

SARIAH: I hope you're right. I could use a break. The last year has been rough.

ROB: This year hasn't been too bad for me, but last year sucked. One of my coworkers was out with his wife when they got hit by a drunk driver. They were both killed. He was one of my best friends, so I'm still not completely over it, though you put one foot in front of the other, you know?

SARIAH: Oh my gosh! I'm so sorry. That sounds horrible.

ROB: It's been over a year now, so it's not as poignant, but at the time, all of us were out of sorts.

SARIAH: I'll bet.

ROB: So I totally understand about having a rough year. All I can say is be kind to yourself. The end of a serious relationship can be like a death in some ways. You have to grieve for your loss.

SARIAH: Have you been through a bad breakup?

ROB: Not in a long time. I travel so much for work, it's hard to meet people and keep up with them. I tend to play the field, to be honest. It's not that I don't want someone special in my life. I've just found it hard to date because of work.

SARIAH: I'm probably too gun-shy for my own good now. Dee is constantly trying to get me to go out, but every time I meet a new guy, I think of Theo. I don't know that I'm ready to give someone else a chance.

ROB: There's no rush. At least, I don't think so. Will you tell me how old you are?

Eeek. This was getting personal. It couldn't hurt, though. Could it?

I hesitated for a few seconds and finally typed my response.

SARIAH: I'm twenty-five. You?

ROB: Twenty-six.

SARIAH: I guess neither of us is in any danger of becoming a spinster. Haha!

ROB: LOL I hope not.

SARIAH: Although guys seem to get more grace in that department. A woman hits thirty and she's past her prime. Men barely peak at thirty.

ROB: True dat. Though I'd like to think I won't peak until well into my fifties.

SARIAH: Very funny.

ROB: I'm kidding. Anyway, I should probably let you get some sleep. Both jobs tomorrow?

SARIAH: Nope, just the day job, and I don't have to go in early. I've hit my sales quota for the week, and they've stopped giving bonuses for going over, so I'd rather sleep in.

ROB: Absolutely. Let me know if you hear about the job, okay? I've got my fingers crossed for you.

SARIAH: I will. And give those pups of yours some love from me.

ROB: They are the most spoiled dogs on the planet. If I give them any more love, they'll probably overdose on it.

SARIAH: Do it anyway!

ROB: Aye aye! Take care.

SARIAH: You too.

I put the phone down and stared up at the ceiling.

This thing with us wasn't real, but it was a nice distraction. It was also nice to have someone to talk to at the end of a long day.

CHAPTER FOUR

Nash

"WHAT AM I DOING, GUYS?" I asked my dogs.

Predictably, there was no response. I set my phone on the kitchen counter and walked over to the fridge, checking my inventory of beer.

Solid. Plus I had more in the garage if I needed it. I was hosting poker night for some of the guys from my team tonight.

I'd gotten distracted from my poker night plans by googling *Sariah* and looking for locals with that name on Facebook. It was fucking dumb for many reasons. Like me, she may not have even told me her real name. Maybe she was smart enough to stay off social media.

Why did I even care? If I wanted a no-strings night in bed, there were plenty of women I could call. *Sariah* could easily be a sixty-year-old Nigerian dude with a solid grasp on the English language, biding his time so he could try to scam me.

In just over an hour, the guys would start showing up at my house and I had beer and water, but I still needed to order pizza and wings. I liked to keep things simple. When Wes hosted poker night, Hadley cleaned the house from top to bottom and put out a massive spread of food.

When I hosted, I relied on my robo-vacuum and Giovanna's Italian Bistro.

I was on my way upstairs to change clothes when my phone started ringing. I jogged back to the kitchen and picked it up off the counter, my jaw tightening with aggravation when I saw that my dad was calling.

"Hey, Dad," I answered stiffly. "What's up?"

"Nash, how are you?"

"I'm fine." I leaned a hip against the counter.

"Nice game the other night. You're on a hot streak."

I stared out at the backyard through the kitchen windows, wishing I'd made it upstairs before I heard my phone ring. So much for my good mood.

"Did you need something?" I asked.

There was a pause before he continued. "Are you going to make it to the anniversary party for your mother and me?"

I looked up at the ceiling and pushed away from the counter. "No, I can't make it."

"Come on, surely you can get away for one evening. Your mother purposely scheduled it on a night you won't have a game, unless you make it to the championship."

"I can't."

A few seconds of awkward silence passed between us before my dad sighed deeply and said, "Nash, your mom misses you."

"I miss her, too. Tell her she should come see me. Anytime."

"But I'm not invited?"

He knew damn well he wasn't invited. My father hadn't been welcome in my life for more than two years. He seemed to think he could just talk his way into a father-son relationship, though. Everything was about appearances to him. After I'd gotten drafted, he'd asked me to secure VIP seating for him and his wealthy investment banking clients for hockey games at my home arena and several others, too. The first couple of years, I'd often join him and his clients for dinner when they were in town, or when I was playing in Chicago.

New York was his favorite, for reasons I hadn't understood when I'd started getting him tickets to those games. Now, he knew better than to even ask.

"I have to go, Dad," I said crisply. "I'm having people over and I've got stuff to do."

"Look, I'm not asking you to come for me. It's for your mother. It would mean the world to her to have all her children at the party."

Nothing was easier for me than saying no to my father. I enjoyed it immensely. But saying no to my mother was a different story. She'd driven me to thousands of hockey practices when I was a kid, and she'd been in the stands cheering me on at every single game I'd ever played. She rarely asked me to do anything, which made it that much harder to disappoint her.

"I'll think about it," I said. "But I have to go."

"Okay, I'll talk to you soon."

I ended the call, scowling at my phone. Whenever I talked to my father next, it would be too soon for me.

———

A FEW HOURS and a few beers later, I was raking in my first poker pot of the night.

"You got lucky," my teammate Boone said, tossing his cards on the table in disgust.

"Bullshit." I grinned as I stacked up my chips. "I'm like a lion in the tall grass, just waiting for my moment to go in for the kill."

My buddy Lars was still shaking his head, looking surprised that he'd lost the hand.

"I was trying for the full house," he said.

I clapped him on the back, his imperfect English making me chuckle.

"Next time," I said. "Or you could just give me your money now and go watch the baseball game."

Preseason baseball had started, and Eric Alvarado was watching a game by himself in my TV room. I was surprised he'd even come over, but I invited the whole team. The other seven guys who'd come were sitting around the custom-made poker table I'd commissioned for nights like this one.

Wes was shuffling the next hand when I picked up my phone and saw a text from Sariah.

SARIAH: Guess what??? I just got a call and I got the job! I can't believe they called me at 7:30 on a Friday night and I can't believe I got the job! It's a lot more money than I was expecting.

·   ·   ·

OKAY, so Sariah wasn't a Nigerian dude, she was definitely a twenty-five-year-old woman and she was definitely cute as hell. I didn't have to see her to know it—I could feel it. I wrote back.

NASH: Congrats! When do you start?

SARIAH: A week from Monday. My current job is cutting back and they don't mind that I'm quitting with only a one-week notice. I'll keep waiting tables until I start, because eating is nice. LOL. What are you up to tonight?

I CONSIDERED what to tell her. If I said I was busy with friends, she'd stop texting me, and who knew how long it would be until she texted me again? I could play poker and text her at the same time. It was Friday night, I didn't have a game, and she had good news to celebrate. Maybe this would be the night I convinced her we should meet up in person. And by *meet up,* I meant screw our brains out later tonight and get to know each other better over breakfast in the morning.

. . .

NASH: Not much. How do you plan to celebrate your good news?

SARIAH: I'm going out for drinks with a friend.

NASH: What's your favorite drink?

SARIAH: I'm a martini girl for sure. What about you?

NASH: I like different beers, but I've been on a porter kick lately.

"HEY, ASSHOLE, YOU PLAYING OR NOT?" Wes demanded from the other side of the poker table.

"He's swiping right on his next elderly dominatrix," Boone cracked as I set my phone down and picked up my cards.

I'd participated in a date auction during a charity event a few months ago and an older woman had bid on an evening with me. And holy shit, what an evening it had been. She'd been dressed in black leather when I'd arrived and I'd not only had to feign interest in her whip collection, but lick her boot so she felt like she got something for the thousands she'd donated to charity. My teammates were never going to let me live it down.

"You getting a spanking from Granny later, Nash?" Drew said, wiggling his brows up and down with amusement.

I put a card on the table and glared at him. "That

joke ran its course, bro. You need to find some new material."

Wes shook his head. "That joke will never run its course, my dude. When we're all retired with great-grandchildren and balls that sag down to our knees, that shit will still be funny."

I ignored him and picked my phone back up as the rest of the table made their bets. Sariah had texted me again and the alcohol in my system made me bolder than usual as I texted her back.

NASH: What are you wearing for your night out?

SARIAH: A slinky little top and a scandalously short skirt.

I SWALLOWED hard and took a sip of my beer, picturing long legs in a skirt that left little to the imagination. And once I started thinking about it, I couldn't focus on anything else.

NASH: Wow. I'd love a pic.

SARIAH: LOL you really don't know me at all. I wouldn't be caught dead in an outfit like that. I'm wearing jeans.

NASH: As long as it's just the jeans and nothing else, I can work with that ;)

SARIAH: You're flirty tonight. Are you drinking?

NASH: I've had a couple beers, yeah. I'm dying to know what you look like.

SARIAH: Why does it matter what I look like?

NASH: You intrigue me. I want to know more.

"Nash, either get your head out of your ass and play, or fold," Wes grumbled. "It's like dealing with my kids. I have to tell you to pay attention a dozen fucking times."

"Annalise listens better than Nash," Lars said.

"Got that right," Wes agreed.

"Fine."

I set my phone down and got my head in the game. A few hands later, we took a break to get drinks and I checked my phone again. Sariah hadn't texted back.

Shit. I'd pushed too hard, asking what she was wearing and what she looked like. She probably thought I was some horny old dude stroking my meat in my basement.

I texted her again.

. . .

NASH: Still there?

I WENT into the kitchen to let my dogs out and to get another beer. Ten minutes later, she'd texted me back.

SARIAH: Just got out of the shower. I have to dry my hair and leave to meet my friend. I promise to send you a pic later

MY SHOULDERS RELAXED as a sense of relief washed over me. Even if Sariah and I never ended up as anything other than friends, I wanted to keep texting her. She was the only person in my life who didn't know that I played professional hockey for a living, the only person who I talked to on a regular basis but had never met. Physical appearance wasn't really part of the equation for us and I'd just fucked that up by asking for a picture of her. I wanted to see if she looked the way I imagined she would, but still felt like I wanted to keep my identity a secret—I knew it was a double standard.

I didn't want her to jump to the same conclusions everyone did when they saw me. Especially women.

They saw an attractive athlete with lots of money, and nothing else about me seemed to matter.

After their romp outside, the dogs had wandered back inside the kitchen area. I grabbed some pizza and wings, and the dogs followed me back to my seat at the poker table, where they all flopped down on the floor to offer me some moral support.

I'd just lost a big hand when I checked my phone and saw a new message from Sariah. She'd attached a picture and I soaked up every detail—a delicate-looking female hand, with manicured nails painted dark purple, was holding a martini glass full of yellow-colored liquid. I couldn't see anything else, but my mood instantly lifted.

"Quit looking at *Grannies Gone Wild*," Wes yelled, tossing a chip at me from the other side of the table.

The chip grazed my ear, but I ignored him.

NASH: Nice. Name the place and I'll be there in ten ;)

SHE WROTE BACK IMMEDIATELY.

SARIAH: Girls only tonight. Another time, Random Rob. That's what my friend calls you.

NASH: Ah, so you're telling your friends about me...
SARIAH: Busted.
NASH: Be good tonight.
SARIAH: You too.
NASH: Always.

CHAPTER FIVE

Sariah

THREE MORE SHIFTS, I told myself as I got home from the restaurant after working a double. My feet hurt, my shoulders were sore, and I smelled like beer. I couldn't wait to run a bath so I could soak in the tub, but I also needed to shower and wash my hair because it probably smelled as bad as the rest of me. I normally came home smelling like food, but one of the new waitresses had spilled a pitcher of beer and half of it landed on me. It was a hassle because it meant I also had to wash a load of laundry tonight.

I was working tomorrow night, Friday night, and the Saturday day shift, and then I was taking Sunday off to relax and prepare for my first day on the job with the Mavericks. I was so excited to start; it was all I'd been thinking about. I'd be working a lot of hours according to my new boss, but it sounded like a lot of fun. The best part was that I wouldn't have to work a strict nine-to-five schedule. I'd be working days, nights, and weekends, depending on the home game schedule, which meant a lot of flexibility. Everything in my life had been pretty structured until now, between college and my job at the paper, so it sounded fun to change things up.

My phone buzzed just as I sank into the steaming hot water in the tub and I stared at Rob's name flashing on the screen of my phone. I still wasn't sure how I felt about this online-type friendship we had going on, but he was funny and kind of sweet. It was nice to talk to someone who didn't seem to want anything from me, despite the uptick in flirting.

ROB: Hey, what's up?

SARIAH: Hi! I'm tired as fuck. I worked a double today at the restaurant and I'm working the next three days too.

ROB: Damn. Well, at least you're raking in the tips, right?

SARIAH: Exactly.

ROB: So...what would you think about talking on the

phone tonight? It would be nice to hear a voice instead of just reading texts.

I chewed my lip as I stared at his message. He already had my number since we were texting, so it couldn't hurt to hear his voice, could it? If he turned into a creep, I could easily block him. Generally speaking, I kept my circle of friends small and my inner circle even smaller. I'd learned a long time ago that drama and backstabbing always followed popularity and I never wanted that to be part of my life again.

Rob wasn't real, though.

It couldn't hurt to talk to someone who sent me sweet pictures of his dogs and occasionally made me laugh.

Could it?

He texted again before I had a chance to respond to the last one.

ROB: Can I sweeten the deal by letting you talk to the gang?

SARIAH: The gang?

ROB: The pups!

SARIAH: Oh, well, in that case, how can I refuse? Go ahead and call. I'm dying to talk to them.

My phone rang almost immediately, and I took a deep breath before answering. "Hi."

"Hey there." His voice was low but well-modulated, with no discernible accent.

"How are you?"

"It's been a busy week."

"Same."

"Okay, so I promised you could talk to the dogs and they're right here. Hang on…" His voice was muffled for a moment. Then I heard him say, "Can you whisper for Sariah? Whisper?"

At first I didn't hear anything, and then a low, short bark greeted me and I laughed with delight.

"Oh my god, that's so cool. Which one is that?"

"That's Athena. She's the best behaved out of the three and the most well trained, although all three of them are really good. She's just super smart. Athena, can you give kisses?"

A moment later I heard a distinct slurping sound and Rob's laughter.

"Okay, don't be jealous, Archie. You can kiss me too."

It went on for about a minute and then Rob came back on the line. "Okay, they've all been given treats and hopefully they'll go to bed now."

"They sound amazing."

"They're a lot of fun. I can't imagine my life without them."

"Must be hard when you travel."

"Sometimes, but I have a pet sitter who takes good care of them."

"That's good."

"So…what are you doing?"

My cheeks flushed as I gazed down at my naked body. "I just got home from work so I'm…in the tub."

"Really?" His voice dropped an octave. "Tell me more."

I chuckled. "Not happening. There have to be rules if we're going to continue to be friends."

"Rules? What kind of rules? I'm not really one for following rules."

"Rules that keep things safe and within boundaries."

"Oh, boy." He huffed out a breath. "Okay, hit me. Let's have them now and get this over with."

"First and foremost, no dick pics. Ever. Like, that's a deal breaker. It's gross and I never, ever want to see something like that."

"Wow, you're no fun at all." His voice was laced with humor, as if trying to hold back laughter. "Go on. What else are you going to break my balls with?"

"You keep the crude remarks and sexual innuendo to a minimum."

"I'm cool with not being crude, but what's wrong with flirting?"

"Nothing, but we don't even know each other. Not really."

"Then let's change that. Tell you what—instead of more rules, how about I promise not to send you risqué pictures of my wiener and we talk instead?"

"Okay. We can do that." I sank lower into the water and closed my eyes. I liked the sound of his voice. It was soothing after a long day listening to loud music and even louder restaurant patrons.

"Tell me something about you that you wouldn't put on the profile of a dating site."

"I would never join one of those," I said quickly. "But if I did, I probably wouldn't talk about my Middle Eastern heritage."

"How come?"

"Well, you know, nine-eleven and all that. If you're Middle Eastern, you're automatically related to Saddam and a terrorist or something."

"That's ridiculous. Were you born there?"

"My parents and siblings and I were all born here in the US, but my father's grandparents came over from Persia back in the 1930s, back before it became Iran. So my father's parents were born there but have been here since they were children. My mother's family is of Persian and Turkish descent, but they've been here for several generations."

"We all came from somewhere else. Unless you're

an American Indian, our ancestors are all from other countries."

"Well, you wouldn't believe how often people say shitty things about the Middle East, so I just don't talk about it. But you asked me to tell you something I don't tell many people."

"I appreciate that."

"What about you?"

"My mother is a mix of Czech and some other eastern European stuff; my father is second-generation Irish."

"Are you close to your parents?"

There was a barely perceptible sigh on his end. "I'm close to my mom, but I don't want to talk about my dad right now. He gives me a headache."

"Are your parents still together or divorced?"

"Still together. What about yours?"

"Yup. My mom rules the roost with an iron fist."

"Are you close?"

"Generally speaking, yes, but since the breakup with Theo, my mom and sisters spend most of their time trying to find me a husband. It can be exhausting to hang out with them these days."

"Believe me, I'm familiar with that." He chuckled. "My mom wants grandbabies so bad she can taste it."

"Do you want kids?"

"Someday? I guess? I can't quite wrap my head around becoming a dad just yet." He paused. "You?"

"Same." I couldn't help but smile to myself. "I think I want them someday, but it's hard to imagine doing what my sister Sophia does. She has a two-year-old and a six-month-old and she never stops. *They* never stop. I'm at her place for ten minutes and kind of start itching to run screaming from the house."

Rob laughed. "Same."

"Don't get me wrong—I love them. They're so cute and rocking the baby to sleep is my favorite thing. But once they're awake and screaming and talking nonstop and pooping...oh my god."

"Ditto. And look how much we have in common."

I chuckled. "Do you spend much time with kids?"

"Actually..." He hesitated. "Remember I told you about my coworker that was killed in the car accident? There's a group of us that have stepped in as honorary uncles, I guess you could call us. We hang out sometimes, babysit once in a while, that kind of thing. Last year, we all dressed up as the Avengers for Annalise's fourth birthday."

My heart clenched, thinking about these two kids I didn't know who'd lost both their parents. "That's very, very sweet of you. You're a nice guy, Random Rob."

He chuckled. "Sometimes. I have other nick-names if you catch me at the right time."

I laughed even as I rolled my eyes. "Well, as fun as that sounds, I'll stick to Random Rob for now."

"For now? Does that mean there's a chance that someday you'll want to meet one of my other personalities?"

"Never say never, but don't get your hopes up."

"Darn."

"Hey, I've enjoyed talking to you but the water's getting cold and I have to get a good night's sleep."

"Wait, I have a question."

"You get one more question, then I have to go to bed."

"If you're Middle Eastern, does that mean you're a brunette?"

I paused. "Are you?"

"I'm more of a dirty blond. If you know what I mean."

I groaned at his lame joke. "Shocker."

"So...brunette?"

"Yes."

"What color eyes?"

"We'll have to save that for next time," I teased. "I can't give away too much all at once."

"You can't blame a guy for trying."

"Good night, Rob."

"Good night, Sariah."

I disconnected the call and took a deep breath, suddenly wondering what Random Rob looked like. Did he look like he sounded—smooth and articulate and sexy? Or was he just a random dude in a basement somewhere catfishing me?

I shook my head and got out of the tub. I couldn't go down that road. I had a busy few days coming up and I planned to read and watch everything I could find about the St. Louis Mavericks. I wanted to know as much as I could before I started on Monday because I was sure there was going to be a steep learning curve. Talking and texting with Rob had been fun, but I probably wasn't going to have much time to talk to him once I started the new job.

Was it weird that I was a little disappointed about that?

CHAPTER SIX

Nash

Eric Alvarado was waiting for me when I walked
into the locker room to change for practice.

"It's not funny," he said, his face twisted in rage.

I scoffed. "Move, dipshit. I need to get changed."

"Not until you promise me your stupid little
tricks are over."

Drew busted out laughing from nearby. I'd
shown him the postcard before mailing it to
Alvarado at his in-laws' house.

"What?" Alvarado demanded, narrowing his eyes
at Drew. "Was it you?"

Drew was the most laid-back guy on the team,

but he was also the Mavericks' oldest veteran player and he didn't take anyone's shit.

"What if it was?" he asked, shrugging. "You need to unclench your ass cheeks if you're going to fit in around here, kid."

Alvarado turned to Wes, who was just walking into the room.

"You're the team captain," he said.

"No shit?" Wes shrugged. "No one ever tells me anything around here. Does that mean I'm getting a raise?"

Alvarado shook his head, looking disgusted. "Why don't you act like a captain and lead? Why do you put up with this shit?"

"What shit are you referring to?" Wes asked as he started to undress and change into his practice clothes.

Sighing dramatically, Alvarado pulled a folded-up postcard from his back pocket and showed it to Wes. Narrowing his eyes, Wes read one side of the postcard out loud.

"Welcome to the Genital Warts Treatment Center. Relief is on the way."

Alvarado had walked right into that one. Everyone within earshot started laughing, and I felt a twinge of pride; I was really bringing my *A* game to this rookie's doorstep.

"Hey Cap," I said, looking at Wes. "I obviously have no knowledge of what's going on here, but I do know that in general, postcards often have something written on the other side, too."

Wes cocked a brow and turned it over, reading the handwritten message on the address side of the postcard.

"Dear Mr. Alvarado, we're sorry to hear about the severe outbreak on your penis, balls, and anus. Please call today and we'll try to move up your next appointment."

The laughter was louder this time, and Alvarado's movements were jerky as he snatched the postcard from Wes's hands.

"I guess I need to go directly to Coach Gizzard about this," he snapped.

"You should," I said, grinning. "Coach loves a good prank. If you could reenact the first time you read it for him, I know he'd appreciate the effort."

I continued getting dressed and as I pulled a clean T-shirt over my head, I found myself being shoved back against my locker.

"Fuck you, Reilly," Alvarado said, pulling his arm back to take a swing at me.

By the time I realized what was going on, Wes and Drew had already pulled him off me. I tugged my T-shirt down, freeing my hands, and advanced toward Alvarado. I was feeling anything but amused.

"No." I heard Lars's voice through the cloud of frustration fogging my brain just as an arm curled around my chest to halt my movements.

Lars had restrained me. I tried to escape his hold, but he was built like a Viking, a wall of solid muscle.

"Let go," I growled, elbowing him in the chest.

He grunted in response, but his hold didn't loosen in the slightest.

"Get him the fuck out of here," Wes told Drew and Boone, pointing at Alvarado.

They dragged a resistant Alvarado to the training room.

"Jesus, he fucking bit me," Boone griped. "The fuck is your problem?"

"This isn't over," Alvarado yelled at me. "We're going to settle this like men."

"Yeah?" I scoffed. "There's only one man here. Who's going to step up for you?"

"Fuck you, Reilly!"

"Go scratch your genital warts, rookie."

Coach Gizzard appeared then, and though his expression was calm, I could tell from the tic in his jaw that he was pissed.

"What the fuck is going on here?" he demanded.

"Nothing we can't handle, Coach," Wes answered.

Coach just shook his head and looked down at the ground, sighing loudly. "I can't believe I have to ask this question, but does someone in this locker room really have genital warts?"

Wes glared at me before answering.

"No, Coach. It was just a prank on the rookie and he doesn't like being pranked."

"Is that so?"

"I've got it under control, Coach," Wes said. "You worry about the important stuff and I'll handle this."

Coach nodded and stalked back to his office.

I elbowed Lars again, trying to get out of his hold. "Will you let go now, fuckface?"

"If you promise not to fight your teammates," he said flatly.

"He pushed me," I said. "I didn't start this."

"Let him go," Wes told Lars.

Lars released me and I scowled at him.

"Look," Wes said to me. "I know he started it, and I know you're not wrong, but we can't bring fighting into this locker room."

I threw my hands up in the air, agitated over this entire conversation. "I didn't start it. He's a fucking hothead baby who needs to be knocked off his pedestal."

Wes put a hand on my shoulder. "I know, man.

I'm going to give him a much different talk than I just gave you."

"I'm not afraid of that little bitch," I muttered.

A smile played on Wes's lips. "I wouldn't expect you to be. Send all the postcards you want, just don't fight the little fucker, okay?"

I shrugged and gave him a shallow nod.

"Don't make me call Mistress Sandra," he said, grinning. "She'll spank the shit out of you."

I couldn't help but laugh at his reference to the bachelor auction from hell and the woman who'd bid on me. I'd figured she was a nice woman I could have dinner and sex with, but instead she had tried to make me her bitch.

I put my hands up. "Okay, Wes, I won't start any more shit with him, but if he initiates anything, I'll finish it."

"I'll talk to him," Wes said. "He needs to save his aggression for out on the ice."

What Wes didn't say was that Alvarado's numbers had been less than stellar since being traded to the Mavericks. That was probably part of the reason he was so wound up. But it was an unwritten rule in hockey that you didn't openly trash a teammate over his on-ice performance unless he did something egregious.

The spotlight was too much for some players.

Those of us who had been at this for a few years knew you had to swallow your pride at times, or your career would be over before you knew it.

I wasn't rooting for Alvarado to fail, but I was still going to prank him. I'd undergone my own trial by fire when I was new to this team, and it had made me stronger.

———

THAT EVENING, I was playing fetch with Louie while scrolling through social media and news articles on my phone when a text notification popped up on my phone.

ALEXA: I bought new lingerie today and I need your opinion on whether it's cute or not...

She was a local, no-strings friend with benefits, though if I was being honest, it was just about the benefits. I really didn't know that much about her. I was pretty sure she was a physical therapist, but that might have been Elle, another woman I hooked up with from time to time.

"Louie, bring me the ball!" I yelled. "C'mon, boy. Bring it back!"

He looked over at me for a second and then took off across my backyard in the other direction. He loved chasing the ball, but I could never get him to bring it back.

Another text alert came through on my phone and I looked down to see a photo from Alexa. She was kneeling on her bed, wearing string bikini panties and a bra so tiny that her tits were spilling over the cups.

She was obviously angling for a hookup. Our casual arrangement had worked well for around eight months now. If we were both free, we got together about once a month, and if we were busy, no hard feelings.

And on the *hard* note, my dick had stiffened in my pants at the sight of her photo. It was basic biology though rather than any connection I had with her; it had been too long since I'd gotten laid and Alexa was always a sure thing.

Another text alert flashed on my phone screen just as I was about to text Alexa back.

SARIAH: Why am I such a horny senior citizen magnet?

Grinning at the screen, I pulled up my text thread with Sariah and responded.

NASH: First I need to understand the question. Are you horny AND a senior citizen magnet, or are you a magnet for horny senior citizens? Fingers crossed you answer this one right.

SARIAH: Ha! Definitely the second. I could have worded that better, right? Horny old men gravitate toward me. I just got a note from an old guy when I went to clear his table. It said: Why would I give you just the tip when I can give you so much more? He also made sure to include his phone number...

NASH: Grandpa's got game!

SARIAH: He looked at least seventy. I read that note and immediately wanted to take a scalding hot shower.

NASH: Did he seriously not tip you and just leave that note?

SARIAH: He seriously did.

NASH: That's fucking crazy!

ALEXA: Hellloooo? Are you leaving me on read???

Shit. I'd forgotten all about Alexa once Sariah had texted.

SARIAH: I hope I never have to waitress again. I'm going to give this new job everything I've got.

Athena and Louie had been chasing after his ball together. She finally stole it away from him and ran over to me, dropping it at my feet and looking up at me expectantly. This was a game they always played when the dogs played fetch together.

"Good girl," I said, rubbing her head.

I threw the ball across the yard and she and Louie took off after it. Then I typed out a quick response to Alexa.

NASH: Hey, sorry. Busy tonight.

I was neither sorry nor busy—I just wasn't feeling it. How many times had I had sex with a woman I didn't know all that well?

More than I'd ever care to admit, and it had been fun most of the time, but also…predictable.

I switched back to my text thread with Sariah again.

NASH: Remind me where the new job is?

SARIAH: If you knew everything about me, the mystery would be gone. What fun would that be?

NASH: Depends. I think it could be a lot of fun ;)

SARIAH: You aren't doing much for my faith in your sex.

NASH: I'm just teasing. Flirting is my second language. Or maybe it's my first?

SARIAH: I'm terrible at flirting.

NASH: Want some lessons?

SARIAH: Would it involve pretending to like photos of your dong?

I laughed as Athena brought me the ball and waited for me to throw it again. It had only taken her a few minutes to steal it this time from Louie, who was keeping his eye on it from nearby.

Sariah wasn't like other women. The more I found out about her, the more she intrigued me. I threw the ball for the dogs again and looked back down at my phone.

NASH: Nope.

SARIAH: You're sweet to offer, but I don't want to get better at batting my eyelashes and laughing at jokes that aren't funny. If a man doesn't like me as I am, he needs to find someone else.

NASH: That's refreshing.

SARIAH: My break is over. Thanks for keeping me company.

NASH: Anytime. Hope you have better luck with customers the rest of the night.

SARIAH: Thanks. I'll settle for getting hit on by guys who aren't on Medicare.

I set my phone down just as Archie waddled over to me and flopped down at my feet.

"Should we get dinner delivered and catch some baseball tonight?" I asked him. "We can order from the place that makes that turkey and vegetable thing you guys like."

He let out a soft *woof* and I gave a scratch behind his ears. I'd surprised myself by picking baseball with my dogs over Alexa tonight, despite my sexual dry spell.

Maybe I just needed a night to decompress. There was no reason to overanalyze it.

CHAPTER SEVEN

Sariah

FOR WHATEVER REASON, I wasn't particularly nervous when I got to the arena for my first day of work. I was calm, centered, and determined. This wasn't just a job; it was my career. One that I'd worked toward since college. Now that I was here, I was one-thousand-percent focused on learning the ropes and starting what I considered to be a new phase of my life. I'd filled out an application for the new apartment I'd been looking at and they'd approved me, so now I had six weeks to pack and get ready to move. I had a direct path to where I was going next in life and it felt good. Almost like being a real grown-up.

Almost.

"You're probably not going to remember the names of all the people you'll meet today," Lance told me as he introduced me to other employees. "But everyone is pretty friendly so I'm sure it won't take long."

"I hope not."

We'd just finished a tour of the executive offices where I'd met everyone from the general manager of the team to head of security for the arena. There were a ton of security protocols, which was nice, but also a little nerve-racking since I had to remember key codes—different ones for different areas—and keep track of a badge. Losing it would cost me a hundred dollars, so I'd be cognizant of that.

"Okay, I have a few things to do before lunch," Lance said. "I'm having food brought in for the sales and marketing team and we're meeting in Conference Room A at noon. We've needed to have one anyway, so I timed it to include you. I know it's your first day, but with us heading to the playoffs, we need to come up with a plan for the summer because I'm positive no matter how far we go, season ticket sales will go up this year. They always do after a playoff run."

I nodded. "Absolutely."

"Okay, I'll see you at noon. The tech guys haven't set up your cubicle or laptop yet, and I'm sorry about that, but it should be done by the end of the day. So until the meeting, please make yourself at home. Wander, get to know the place, talk to people—and I apologize again for not having your station set up."

"It's no problem." I smiled. "I can entertain myself until it's time for lunch."

"Great." He smiled back and headed in the other direction.

I liked him as far as bosses went. Obviously, I didn't know him very well but he was about forty, seemed to know a lot about both hockey and St. Louis, and while friendly, he was all business. I figured I could learn a lot from him.

I decided to make a quick trip to the ladies' room now, while I technically didn't have anything to do. I headed down the hall and paused in front of that damn picture of a half-naked Nash Reilly. He was insanely good-looking. Not my type, but there was no mistaking his appeal. He was broad shouldered with a set of abs that could make women clench in anticipation. If there was one thing about him that was my type, it was his biceps. I loved firm, rounded biceps on a man, and while I couldn't touch a picture, I had a feeling his whole body was firm.

"He's pretty, right?" A gorgeous dark-skinned woman came to stand behind me, her eyes following mine.

"I'm just amazed that a pro hockey player would do an underwear ad," I said, chuckling.

"It's been nothing but good press for the team," she replied, grinning. "Ticket sales are through the roof since that ad came out. As if women think they're going to get close to him just by coming to the games."

"Are you in the sales department?" I asked her.

"No, I'm the video coordinator," she replied, holding out her hand. "Monique Devereaux."

"Hi. I'm Sariah Ansari. Today is my first day."

"Welcome!" Monique's smile was warm and friendly. "This is a great place to work. And the eye candy doesn't hurt." She glanced in the direction of Nash's picture and we both laughed.

"I'm not really here for eye candy," I said. "But it's nice to look at now and again."

"Well, I've been married for fifteen years and I'm always here for the eye candy. That's why it's called *eye* candy—because we can look without touching."

"I guess you have a point."

"Are you heading for the ladies' room? Because I have to go."

"Yes, I was." We continued in that direction. "So, what exactly does a video coordinator do?" I asked.

"I collect and..." She paused, chuckling. "*Coordi-nate* all the video taken during games and any other official events. I make cuts to send to the coaches for when they want to go over games or specific plays, I make different versions for events and commercials, stuff like that. That's the general gist of my job."

"Are you a big hockey fan?"

She laughed. "Believe it or not, I'm from New Orleans, where we don't know hockey from curling, but I dated a hockey player in college and I was hooked."

"Is that your husband?"

"No. Just a guy I dated for about six months. But it was enough to make me fall in love with the sport. What about you?"

"Honestly, I didn't know much about it until the last year or so, watching the team. Then I was hooked." We went into separate bathroom stalls, continuing to talk as we did our business.

"Hockey is exciting," she said. "I love watching. I love going to the games. I love the team, to be honest. The guys are great. And Nash is my buddy."

"He is?" I asked in surprise.

"There's more to the man than a pretty face. He's a prankster, though, always pulling shit on his teammates. And sometimes me, but he knows I can send doctored videos to the whole team showing him doing anything I want, so we've come to an understanding." Her voice was filled with amusement.

"That sounds…intense."

"No, not at all." She laughed. "I'm mostly kidding. We do bust each other's chops, especially on the road, but—"

"You travel with the team?"

"Oh, yeah." Her voice softened. "I love it, but it's hard at home sometimes. My husband is an accountant, so he never goes anywhere but to work. He's a homebody. I'm the opposite."

"They say opposites attract, right?"

We came out of our stalls within a few seconds of each other and our eyes met in the mirror as we washed our hands. "Damn straight they do." She fixed me with a gorgeous smile and it was infectious.

"Anyway, I have to get some work done," she said as we got back into the hall. "Once you get your bearings around here, come find me and we'll do lunch later this week."

"That sounds awesome. It was nice to meet you."

"Likewise." She headed in the opposite direction and I went in search of my cubicle, even though I couldn't get much work done yet.

Lance had said he wanted me to sit with a different sales guy for a few hours every day this week. That way I'd get a feel for the different styles and personalities, as well as how they did things around here.

"Hi. Sariah, right?" An older man, who looked to be in his late fifties, came over holding out his hand. "I'm Kevin Gerard. You'll be sitting with me this afternoon, after our lunch meeting."

"Nice to meet you." We shook hands. "I'm not sure who Lance wanted me to sit with."

"He just sent me an email. So come on over to my desk and I can show you a few shortcuts I use."

"Great." I followed him. I was enjoying the vibe here; professionalism tempered with friendliness and a laid-back attitude.

We spent about forty minutes going over the basics of the different season ticket packages and had just stood up to go to lunch when a couple of guys came into the office. One was holding a hockey stick and he approached Kevin.

"Hey. Here's the stick you asked for. The whole team signed it, as requested."

"Thanks, Wes. Appreciate that." Kevin nodded and turned to me. "This is Sariah; she's new to the sales team. Sariah, this is Wes Kirby, the captain of the team."

"Nice to meet you, Mr. Kirby." His hand was warm and dry as we shook.

"Welcome," he said to Kevin, his eyes crinkling a little as he smiled. He turned to look back at me and said, "Nice to meet you too, but please—it's Wes."

"Okay, then. Wes."

"This stick is for a customer who just bought season tickets for next year," Kevin told me. "He wants to give it to his son for his birthday this weekend and this is how I clinched the deal. Luckily, the guys are great about doing stuff like this."

"Anything you need," Wes said to me. "If we can do it and it helps the team, just reach out. And please don't stand on ceremony here. Kevin has my cell number. Get it from him and let me know how I can help close a deal. I know it can be a little intimidating in the beginning, but don't hesitate to call me."

"Wes—you comin' to lunch or what?" A voice called out.

I turned just as Nash freakin' Reilly came into the room.

Oh, hell, he was even better looking in person. With his blond hair wet and a pair of low-slung sweats on beneath a Henley that pulled tight across his shoulders, it took me a second to stop staring. For a guy who wasn't my type, he was breathtaking. My heart actually skipped a beat when I saw him and that was so unlike me. My entire body was on high alert, as if he'd actually touched me.

What the hell was that about?

"Keep your pants on," Wes called back to Nash. "I'm—"

He was cut off as one of the media relations guys caught sight of Nash. "Nash, come here! I need you, man."

"What's up?" Nash turned and walked into one of the offices.

"I guess I'll introduce you to Nash next time," Wes said to me. "And if you want to meet the team, just have Lance check with Coach and we'll find a time after a practice or something."

"It's good to be familiar with everyone," Kevin added. "Especially when you have a customer who wants something signed or whatever."

I nodded. "Thank you. I appreciate it."

"I'm gonna use the restroom," Kevin said as Wes headed in the other direction. "See you in the conference room."

"See you." I grabbed a pen and paper since I didn't have a company laptop yet, along with my purse, and headed in the direction of Conference Room A.

I pulled out my phone for the first time all day as I walked.

I'd missed a call from my mother. Big surprise. She knew I was starting a new job but still probably wanted to chat about who I was and wasn't dating.

I also had four texts.

I opened the messaging app and smiled at the one from Dee.

DEE: Kick ass and take names today! I want all the deets when you get home! Love you!

I decided not to text her back until later since I didn't have much time.

There was a text from Sophia, also wishing me luck, and the last two were from Rob.

ROB: Hope you have an amazing first day!

ROB: If you have a chance, drop me a quick text and let me know how it's going. I'm sure you're going to do great. Also, the canine gang says good luck!

And he'd attached a photo of all three dogs sitting at his feet, mouths open, tongues hanging out. It was absolutely adorable, and I couldn't help but smile.

SARIAH: It's been a great day so far! Heading into a lunch meeting. Not sure what time I'll be home, but I'll try to call later.

CHAPTER EIGHT

Nash

"I LIKE TEAMWORK, BOYS," Coach Gizzard said, his tone overly cheerful. "It gives me the warm fuzzies. Reminds me of drinking cocoa with my dearly departed grandma in front of a fire."

We were fucked. There wasn't a single doubt in my mind that after the disastrous road trip we'd just had, there would be a price to pay at practice today.

"Hey, Coach Seville, what's that other thing I like?" Gizzard asked one of his assistant coaches, whose expression was stoic.

"You like making the playoffs, Coach," Seville said.

"That's it!" Gizzard grinned, continuing his

charade. "And you know, I've almost forgotten what it feels like to make the playoffs." He scanned each of our faces. "Do you boys remember what it feels like to make the playoffs?"

I shifted my weight to my other side, not daring to make eye contact with any of my teammates.

Coach was right. On the verge of clinching a playoff spot, we'd choked on our last road trip. We'd lost every game. As Sariah and I texted every evening about the new job she'd started a week ago, she'd asked me how my job was going. I told her it was a stressful time, but I couldn't reveal much more without telling her I was a hockey player. She wasn't ready for us to reveal those kinds of details to each other. I'd come close to telling her anyway, because it had been a hard fucking week.

"Hey, Coach," Gizzard called out. "Are there any pucks in that bag today?"

Groans echoed around the arena as Coach Seville reached down and picked up the bag at his side. You didn't play hockey for most of your life without knowing exactly where our head coach was going with today's practice.

Seville opened the bag and looked inside. "It's empty, Coach."

"Not a single puck in that bag!" Coach Gizzard boomed. "I wonder how we can stop playing like a bunch of pimply junior leaguers who care more about jerking off than winning if we don't have a single puck?"

He stopped and scanned our faces, and I schooled my expression into a mixture of concern and remorse. There was literally no worse time to roll your eyes or look disinterested than this.

"Want to bag skate 'em, Coach?" Coach Seville asked.

Coach Gizzard snapped his fingers and pointed at the assistant coach. "That's a great idea, Coach Seville! Let's bag skate these highly paid, unmotivated junior leaguers until they remember how the fuck to dig deep and win games!"

"On the line!" Seville called, blowing his whistle.

Hell. I hadn't been bag skated in *years*. Coaches reserved this punishment for a reason—it was physically and mentally exhausting. There was a solid chance I'd be puking up my breakfast by the end of this.

Collectively, though, we deserved this. Coach Gizzard was right—we made too much money to play like we had on our road trip. We also had more pride in ourselves than that. The loss of our former team captain, Ben Whitmer, had hit us all hard and we honored him by winning.

Coach Gizzard brought his *A* game to the bag

skate, making us come to a full stop on the lines because it was harder. We skated line drills and laps, followed by more line drills and more laps.

"This is bullshit," Boone murmured while his mouth was hidden behind his water bottle during a thirty-second water break.

"Shut the fuck up," I murmured back.

As soon as we started skating again, Lars and Eric quickly had to stop to vomit up the water they'd just drank.

"How long does it take to puke?" Coach yelled out. "Get your ass moving, Alvarado!"

My entire lower body hurt by the time we were done. Konstantin Volkov, our backup goalie, fell to his knees on the ice, completely gassed.

"You wanted to quit an hour ago, but did you?" Coach called out. "Next game I better see every one of you skating like you're being chased by a goddamned axe murderer and fighting for that puck like your opponents just fucked your mothers, you hear me?"

"Yes, Coach," we said in unison.

I hadn't puked during the drills, but I felt everything I'd eaten or drank coming up now. I knew better than to interrupt my coach, though. Someone had brought a stack of buckets out to the ice for those that had to puke, and I was just going over to grab one when Coach waved toward the locker room.

"Get your asses out of here! We're doing this after every game someone slacks in, so you may want to order your own buckets with unicorns and hearts on them for next time."

I hadn't seen our head coach so pissed in a long time. It probably had something to do with his job being on the line if we didn't make the playoffs for a second year in a row.

The pressure was always on for all of us. When people commented that it must be fun to play a game for a living, they never seemed to consider that we weren't just expected to *play* the game. We needed to consistently *win* it.

I ran the last twenty feet to the locker room, barely making it to a trash can in time. My body didn't quit until I'd puked up every bit of food and water I'd had today.

When I stood back up, Josh, one of our trainers, was next to me. He passed me a wet hand towel and said, "Meet me in the training room."

I nodded, wiped my face off and tossed the towel in a laundry bin on the way into the training room.

It felt good to lie down on a padded massage table. Tony put a pillow beneath my head and gave me some Gatorade to sip while he stretched out my legs. I felt myself sliding into sleep.

It wouldn't hurt to give in to a quick nap.

———

I woke up and swiped the back of my hand across my mouth to wipe away a little drool.

The lights were off in the training room. Through the light streaming in from the window in the door, I could see two other guys were asleep in here, too. Someone had covered all of us up.

Looking down at my watch, I saw that it was two thirty p.m. Wow. I'd slept for a couple of hours.

When I slid off of the table to the floor, my sore legs immediately reminded me of the grueling bag skate. My stomach was painfully empty but I still felt like eating might make me sick again.

I quietly left the room and headed for the shower. By the time I finished rinsing off and got some clean clothes on, I felt like myself again.

There was no one left in the locker room, so I'd be having lunch alone. Probably for the best. I'd just pick something up and take it home in case I got sick again.

But first, I had to stop by the front office to talk to our team's video coordinator, Mo. I'd watched the footage of the games she'd compiled for me on our road trip, but she always liked to talk to the players after she'd had a chance to watch it all herself.

When I walked into the front office, Mo was talking to one of the receptionists. She gave me a bright smile.

"Nash, you busted me."

"Hey, Mo." I looked at the receptionist. "Hey, Carly."

Mo looked at the donut in her hand. "I'm supposed to be on a diet, but these donuts have been calling my name from the break room."

"I'm pretty sure you deserve that donut, Mo."

"Damn right I do. You guys have been keeping me busy."

I sighed and shook my head. "Lots of stupid mistakes to analyze from our last few games."

She furrowed her brow in a look of sympathy. "I heard you guys had a rough practice this morning."

I nodded. "Hope you don't have to watch video of that one; it wasn't pretty."

"Do you want a donut?"

"I'd love one, thanks."

"Jelly filled or glazed?"

I considered my choices. "I'll go with glazed."

"Be right back."

"How's it going, Carly?" I asked as Mo walked toward the break room.

"Good. Hey, I don't mean to bug you, but do you think you could sign a photo for my niece? She thinks you're the cat's pajamas."

I laughed heartily at that. "High praise. Of course I will."

She got up and walked over to a wall of cabinets, where she took out a box of photos. It was, of course, one of the photos from the photo shoot I did for the sexiest athlete article. I signed and personalized at least twenty-five of them a week, and when the front office needed me to, I'd sign just my name on a stack of at least one hundred of them.

"Nash!" One of the sales guys, Kevin Gerard, called out to me as I signed the photo for Carly's niece.

"Hey, man. How's it going?" I said, passing the photo to Carly.

Kevin was a good dude. I'd attended several lunches with him as a perk for fans that bought premium season ticket packages and VIP boxes.

"Can't complain." He shook my hand and gestured behind him. "Nash, I want to introduce you to our newest sales employee, Sariah Ansari."

Sariah? My heart pounded at the mention of the name. It was unusual, but was I jumping to conclusions for thinking it might be the same Sariah I'd been texting with?

A beautiful brunette approached, smiling and offering me her hand.

"Hi, Nash. It's great to meet you," she said.

I was momentarily speechless. *Holy shit, please let this be the same Sariah I've been talking to.*

With an olive complexion and golden-brown eyes, she drew me in without even trying. I had to find out if this was the woman I was slowly getting to know.

"Sariah, great to meet you," I said, shaking her hand. "How long have you been with the team?"

"About a week now."

"Really?" I arched a brow, mentally ticking one box. "And what did you do before?"

"I worked in sales for a weekly newspaper and waitressed."

Bingo. It was all I could do not to show how excited I was. Fuck, I was *thrilled*. I already liked her just from the conversations we'd had, and now I knew she was legitimately who she said she was. She was also gorgeous.

Did she feel the same attraction I did? Surely she did.

"Nice," I said.

"Sariah is working on selling her first corporate box," Kevin said.

"Perfect. I'm sure you'll have no trouble."

"Actually," she said. "I could use your help."

The pieces were falling into place. I'd join her and the prospective VIPs for lunch and find a way to get some time alone with her.

"Of course. What can I do?" I said, trying to play it cool.

"Can you sign a few…undies photos?" she asked, a light pink flush appearing on her cheeks.

I grinned. "You like the undies ones better than the ones in my uniform?"

"No, it's not that. The CEO I'm trying to close the deal with has a daughter. He wants them for her and her friends."

Hmm. I didn't like how quickly she'd said *no*. Most women went nuts over those pictures.

"Absolutely, whatever you need," I said. "You want me to sign one for you, too?"

Sariah burst out laughing. It wasn't a nervous laugh, either. It was a full-throated, *that's fucking hilarious* kind of laugh. Kevin gave her a sideways look and she covered her mouth with her hand, looking a little embarrassed to be caught laughing.

"That's um, really generous of you," she said.

"Thank you. But we'd better save the photos for fans and clients."

The front office ordered those photos by the thousands, but I was too aggravated to mention it.

"I'll take one, Nash," Carly offered. "You're my mom's favorite player. I know she'd love one."

At least Carly's mom had good taste. Sariah obviously did not.

"Hey, we have to head out on a sales call," Kevin said. "Nash, if you go into my office, there's a Post-it right next to the keyboard with the names of the people we need those photos personalized for."

"I'll do it before I leave here," I said.

"Great to meet you, Nash," Sariah said, waving.

"You, too."

Right after they left, Mo returned with my donut. I thanked her and took a huge bite, trying to not sulk.

Apparently, Sariah wasn't a huge fan of my underwear ad. Between that and the bag skate, I was in a shitty mood now. I just wanted to go home, where I was actually appreciated.

Even if it was only by my dogs.

CHAPTER NINE

Sariah

"Auntie Sariah!" My two-year-old niece, Reva, came running toward me as I walked into my sister Sophia's house. I hadn't been here in over a month and I scooped her up, kissing the side of her face.

"Hey, Revy-Levy-Mevy."

She giggled at the ridiculous nickname she'd given herself. It was our little joke because her parents and grandparents refused to use it, but I thought it was sweet and silly. Just like her.

"I wish you wouldn't call her that." Sophia gave me a look.

"She's two, Sophie." I scowled back at her. "If she can't be a little silly now, then when?"

"You'll see when you have your own kids," she said, lifting her chin a little. "You want to instill good habits and memories from the very beginning."

I was extremely proud of myself for not rolling my eyes. I did it far too often with Sophia because she was everything I wasn't, according to my mother, and I heard about it constantly when we were together.

Today was Sunday. I'd been working for the Mavericks for two weeks and this was my first day off. The team was out of town and I was grateful to have nothing going on. After closing the deal on my first corporate box, I felt like I deserved an entire weekend off. I'd spent yesterday doing laundry and cleaning my apartment because I'd known I was expected at family dinner today. The plan was to spend a couple of hours with everyone, eat, and then head home so I could get to bed early. The coming week was going to be busy once the team got back from their road trip on Tuesday.

"Do you need help with anything?" I asked Sophia. No one else had arrived yet so I figured I'd do what I could.

"Just keep Reva out of my hair," Sophia replied, heading toward the kitchen. "Felipe is putting the baby down for his nap, so if I can have thirty uninterrupted minutes, everything will be ready by the time people get here."

"Okay." I put a wriggling Reva down and she instantly grasped my hand, pulling me toward the family room and the massive toy box that lived there.

"Dollies!" she announced happily.

"Okay." I put down my purse and kicked off my shoes before sitting cross-legged on the floor with her. She handed me a Barbie and picked up Ken.

"Daddy!" she said.

"Which one is Mommy?" I asked.

Reva picked up another Barbie dressed in a Cinderella-like gown, complete with a tiara on her head. "Mama!"

I managed not to laugh since that was a pretty astute description of my sister, even now that she was married with two kids.

Glancing up at the fireplace, my eyes settled on a picture my mother called the proudest moment of her life. In a beautiful gilded eight-by-ten frame was a photograph of me, Sophia, and Sami, our other sister. Sophia had just crowned Sami Miss Missouri —Sophia had won the year before—and I was there in my capacity as Miss Teen Missouri. Three beauty queens, smiling for the cameras.

I momentarily shuddered at the memories.

I hated everything about that time in my life and after graduating from high school a year later, I'd left the world of modeling and pageants forever. Much to my mother's chagrin. I was pretty sure she still hadn't forgiven me.

"Did you get my email about Sami's engagement party? It's next month." Sophia called to me from the kitchen, startling me out of my reverie.

"There's potentially a playoff game that day," I replied. "I don't know if I'll be able to make it until the end of the regular season." I mentally cringed, waiting for the storm to hit.

"What the hell are you talking about?" Sophia came into the room wiping her hands on a dish towel, her dark eyes flashing.

"I have a job, Sophie." I met her gaze squarely.

"You can ask for a day off!" she hissed, hands on her hips.

"Not during the playoffs."

"That's ridiculous."

"It's not. It's a busy time. And maybe I can get the evening off, but I can't give you a firm answer until the season is over."

She glared at me. "Mom is going to have an aneurysm."

I blew out a frustrated breath. "I can't help that."

Luckily, Sami and her fiancé Sebastian arrived,

calling out to us and effectively ending the conversation. For now, anyway. It was bound to come up again when my mom got here.

"Sam-Sam!" Reva got up and ran to her aunt. She had nicknames for almost everyone in the family, another thing that annoyed Sophia to no end.

My parents arrived a few minutes later, followed by my grandmother, aunt, and uncle, all on my father's side. Sami carried a stack of bridal magazines with her, setting them on the living room table as we all exchanged greetings.

"I've found the perfect wedding dress!" she announced.

"Already?" I asked.

She nodded. "It's sheer perfection. I can't wait to show you."

"After dinner," Mom said, air-kissing me and then scooping Reva up off the floor.

"How's Grandma's girl?"

She carried her off as Sebastian gave me a grin. "How's the job with the Mavericks?"

"It's great," I told him. Seb was a huge hockey fan, so he'd been the most excited of anyone when I'd gotten the job. "When do you want to come to a game?"

He shrugged. "Sami isn't interested so I'm not sure."

"I'll go with you." My father surprised me by coming to join us. "I like hockey."

"You do?" I asked suspiciously. Since when? My dad watched a little football, but he was far more interested in European soccer.

"I love sports," he said easily. "Just wasn't a priority over the years. Now that I'm older, I'm enjoying life a little more. Going to a hockey game with my future son-in-law sounds like fun."

"Let me know and I can get you tickets," I murmured.

"Hockey is awful," Sami said, wrinkling her nose. "All that fighting. Yuck."

"It's not all fighting," I protested. "And anyway, the guys I've met have been really great. Helpful, polite, generally good guys."

"Yeah, like that underwear model?" Sami snickered. "Does he parade around the office like that?"

I frowned. "Nash? Of course not. None of the guys parade around the office." For some reason, hearing her mocking the team felt like a jab at my new job. It shouldn't have bothered me, because this was nothing new, but it did.

"Is he as hot as he is in the pictures or is it all Photoshop?" she asked.

"He's very handsome in person," I admitted. "I don't think they photoshopped much."

"But is he nice?" she asked, wiggling her eyebrows.

I rolled my eyes. "He's always been polite the times I've met him, but I don't really know him."

"What underwear model?" Dad asked.

Sami smirked, pulling out her phone and typing something in. Then she turned it around to show our father. "This guy plays for the Mavericks. Can you believe it?"

"He probably makes a shit ton of money," Seb said, glancing at the photo and shrugging. "I'd do it if someone wanted to pay me for pictures of me in my worn-out Fruit of the Loom boxers!"

"Over my dead body!" Sami said, laughing and nudging him with her shoulder. He nudged her back and they exchanged a long, sweet look that made me turn my attention to my dad.

"Anyway, if you want to go to a game, just let me know."

"Thank you." Dad put a gentle hand on my arm when they walked away. "Don't listen to them. I'm very proud of you for getting such an amazing, high-profile job. Did you close the deal for the corporate box?"

I nodded. "I did." Ironically, my somewhat old-fashioned Middle Eastern father was far more interested in my career than my mother or sisters.

"I knew it." He grinned, his hazel eyes crinkling with pleasure.

"Thanks, Dad." I smiled as my mother came into the room.

"You work with an underwear model? What nonsense is this?"

I sighed.

———

Dinner was long and arduous. I loved my family. I really did. I just didn't understand this need to nitpick every aspect of my life, especially the personal parts. Mom had three dating prospects lined up, all vetted and waiting to hear from me. I gave her a firm no before retreating into the family room to play with Reva.

"Mom's just trying to help," Sophia said, following me with seven-month-old Thomas in her arms. She sank into a chair to feed him and eyed me curiously. "I understand you're bitter about the breakup with Theo, but you need to get back out there."

"I need to focus on my mental health, my career, and moving," I corrected her gently. "I can't be happy with someone else until I'm happy being on my own."

"And you're not happy on your own?"

"I've been working two jobs since the breakup to be able to afford the apartment he left me in. Once I move and pay off a little debt, then maybe I'll be relaxed enough to think about dating."

Sophia sighed but nodded. "I guess you know what's best. Just don't deprive yourself of finding someone wonderful because Theo was an ass."

"I'll try not to."

My phone buzzed in my pocket and I was pleasantly surprised to see a message from Rob. We hadn't talked much the last week, which was kind of weird, but he'd said his travel schedule was crazy.

ROB: Hey, how was family dinner?

SARIAH: I'm still here. Food was good and my niece is hilarious. On the flip side, my sister's engagement party is coming up and I don't know if I'll be able to go because of work. It's made me incredibly popular here today.

ROB: You can't get the time off?

SARIAH: I'm brand new. I don't feel comfortable asking for time off this soon.

ROB: I think most jobs would understand, especially on a weekend.

SARIAH: I'll talk to my boss this week.

ROB: How's work going in general?

SARIAH: It's pretty great. I closed a big deal just

recently, which is going to mean a nice bonus. I'm super excited and I think my boss was impressed.

ROB: Good for you. Congrats!

SARIAH: Thanks.

ROB: So, do you like it there?

SARIAH: I've made friends and everyone is cool, so I'm happy with the way things are going. There's a woman named Monique who cracks me up every damn day. She's hilarious. And my boss is pretty laid back, which is a nice change from my old boss at the newspaper.

ROB: Sounds like you've settled in.

SARIAH: I think so. At least I don't hate waking up in the morning because I don't want to go to work. In fact, it's the opposite. I never know what's going to happen, which is pretty cool.

ROB: Sounds like a fun place to work.

SARIAH: Don't get me wrong, it's intense. There's a lot of money at stake, and pressure to sell sell sell, but it's invigorating instead of draining. It's hard to explain.

ROB: I think I know what you mean.

SARIAH: Ugh. I have to go. I'm getting the stink eye from my mom for being on my phone. Meanwhile, my sisters, my eighty-year-old grandmother, and sixty-year-old aunt are giggling over pictures of one of the guys I work with.

ROB: Huh?

SARIAH: One of my coworkers does some modeling

on the side and my sister pulled it up on her phone to show everyone. Now they're giggling like teenagers.

ROB: You're not into models?

SARIAH: Those kinds of guys have wayyyy too much ego and emotional baggage for me. I prefer a boyfriend with more body hair than I have. Trust me, I would know.

ROB: I'm intrigued. Did you used to date a model?

SARIAH: Unfortunately, that's a long story and I have to go before my mother turns me into a pillar of salt with one of her glares. Maybe we can talk one night this week?

ROB: Sure. I'll be home in a few days and it won't be as stressful at work.

SARIAH: Great. Talk soon!

CHAPTER TEN

Nash

"How is this possible?" Lars asked me, arching a brow skeptically.

"I know, dude. It's weird that it happened this way, but it did. The woman I've been texting is definitely the new woman in sales."

We were at a downtown St. Louis bar having lunch, and I'd made a spur-of-the-moment decision to tell Lars about my dilemma. He was hung up on how unlikely it was that the person who had randomly texted me was now working for our team.

"It sounds like a scam," he said, his face twisting into an expression of suspicion.

"How could it be a scam? She's not asking me for anything."

"Not now, but..." He shrugged. "Sheridan and I just watched a movie on Netflix about a man who scammed women out of money using dating apps."

I shook my head before continuing.

"It's definitely not a scam, bro. And that's not even why I told you. Can you rewind to the part where I asked you for advice on whether I should tell her who I am?"

"Of course you should tell her."

Everything was black and white to Lars, which meant sometimes his advice was great, but other times...not so much.

"She laughed at my ad photo. I don't think she'll like finding out I'm the guy she's been texting."

His lips tilted up into a small smile. "If she laughed at your photo, then I like her. You should try to make this work. Don't screw it up like you always do."

I glared at him, about to fire off a response when a man approached our table.

"Excuse me, but you're Lars Jansson, right?"

"Yes."

The man's whole face lit up. "I'm a huge Mavericks fan. I hate to impose, but do you think I could get a photo with you?"

"Of course," Lars said. "Do you want Nash in the photo, too?"

The man looked at me, confusion on his face. "Nash Reilly?"

"Guilty." I flashed a grin at him and the woman standing next to him.

"Sorry I didn't recognize you," the fan said. "That'd be great to have both of you in the picture."

"You did not recognize him because of the clothes," Lars said. "You are used to seeing him with just his underwear."

The man laughed as he passed his phone to the woman at his side. "Oh yeah, the underwear ad. I see that picture everywhere I go. I can't believe I didn't recognize you."

My teammates never missed a chance to make fun of me for the ad, even Lars. But when it was his turn to be the butt of a joke, he had no sense of humor.

We posed for the photo, shook the fan's hand, and went back to our lunch.

"I have a better chance of getting to know her if I just don't say anything," I said.

He arched a single brow again, his trademark move. "How are you getting to know each other if she doesn't know who you are?"

I shrugged. "She's still getting to know me. She just thinks I'm Rob."

"Who is Rob?"

"That's the fake name I gave her when we first started texting."

Lars looked up from his food and made eye contact with me. "What is the word for when someone does things on purpose to make them fail?"

English wasn't his first language, and I regularly helped him with rarely used words and phrases.

"Being your own worst enemy?"

He shook his head.

"Sabotage?"

"Yes, that is it. Every time you really like someone, you sabotage it."

I balked. "Bullshit. I do not, and you don't even understand what I'm saying. I *just* found out she's the woman I've been texting. It's not like I could have told her in front of Kevin from sales."

"You could have told her that evening, by calling her. Did you?"

"Where's our server? I need more iced tea."

Lars cleared his throat. "I asked you a question—did you?"

I scowled at him. "Don't ask questions you already know the answer to, douchebag. Would we be sitting here talking about whether I should tell her if I'd already told her?"

"Why didn't you tell her?"

I scanned the restaurant for our server, grumbling. "A person could die of thirst around here."

"You're avoiding the core question in this discussion," Lars said matter-of-factly.

"You know, you're a real pleasure to talk to since you started therapy. Always trying to analyze everything."

He shrugged. "Why meet around the bush?"

"It's *beat* around the bush, asshole."

"That sounds dirty."

The server came by our table with an iced tea refill for me and after I thanked her and took a sip, I said, "I already told you why. It's because I don't think she'll like me."

"So what? Then you can move on to someone else who will."

"Will they, though? I've been thinking since I met Sariah about how many women have actually really known me. I know they pretend I'm the greatest thing ever, but...in reality, they just see good looks and money and try to be what they think I want."

Lars nodded. "I've felt that way about women before, too. Before Sheridan, I mean."

I finished my lunch and pushed my plate aside.

"When Sariah and I are texting, I get to see who she really is. And I get to be honest about who I really am."

Lars gave me an *are you really being honest* look, but I put up a hand to keep him from commenting.

"Other than my name," I said. "And a few other key details, I guess. But you know what I mean. I'm not a pro hockey player or a hot underwear model when I'm talking to her. I'm just *me*. I've never had that before and it feels good."

Lars leaned back and crossed his arms, considering my situation. "You don't want to hear my advice."

"You of all people should know what I'm saying. That it's nice to be liked for who you are instead of what you do and what you have."

His smile was wry. "You always give me the advice I don't want, so I will do the same. Being a pro hockey player with money and good looks *is* part of who you are. You should either never tell her, and only be text friends, or tell her immediately."

"Those things aren't part of who I am though," I argued. "They don't really matter."

"Any woman who dates you is dating someone who is on the road a lot. Someone who has willing women waiting in every city. Many women want to date a hockey player, until they're dating a hockey player."

I'd seen that time and again with my teammates and experienced it myself, too. There was no way to know if Sariah was like that, but one thing I was sure about was that knowing my identity would change how she felt about me.

"I just need more time to show her who I really am," I said. "I don't plan to keep her in the dark forever."

Lars's smile was knowing. "If I did this to Sheridan, when I finally told her who I was, she'd cut off my ball sac and mount it on her wall like a deer head."

"Yeah, she'd be pissed," I agreed.

My phone dinged with a text alert. I read it and then showed it to Lars.

SARIAH: My new job takes me to lots of cool places and today I'm at a hockey arena. Have you ever smelled hockey gloves? Not when they're new, but after they've been worn? They smell worse than a rotting corpse.

He smiled. "Here's your chance. Tell her you smell them all the time. Tell her she probably just smelled yours."

I gave him a look and texted her back.

NASH: I can't say I have. Are you in a locker room?

SARIAH: I was earlier.

NASH: Were there naked dudes in there?

SARIAH: God no. No players at all.

NASH: Anyone you wish you'd seen naked in the locker room?

"What are you saying to her?" Lars asked.

I showed him my phone screen and he groaned. "This will not end well, Nash."

I scoffed. "Why? You think she's going to say you?"

"It would be weird for me if she did. I'd think of it every time I saw her."

SARIAH: That's a weird question. No, I can't think of anyone I wish I'd seen naked. The whole world has pretty much seen one of the guys from the team who uses this arena naked—he did an underwear ad!

I smiled at the phone screen. Now we were getting somewhere.

NASH: Hey, that's pretty cool. He must have a killer body.

SARIAH: If you like waxed chests and airbrushing. He's not my type. I can tell just by looking at the photo that he's arrogant.

I lowered my brows and muttered, "What the fuck?"

"I told you," Lars said, giving our server his debit card for the check.

NASH: Have you met him?

SARIAH: Once. He offered to sign one of his photos for me. HARD PASS. LOL. What the hell would I do with an underwear photo?

Ouch.

SARIAH: Anyway, how's your day going?

NASH: Not bad. Just had lunch with a friend.

SARIAH: Speaking of lunch, mine's almost over. I'm going out for drinks with a coworker after work tonight so I won't be home until late. Text tomorrow when you can.

I practically growled at her response. That douchebag Kevin was making a move on her already. I just knew it. Fucker.

NASH: So you already have a friend at work? That's nice.

SARIAH: I must not be making a horrible impression. We'll see how tonight goes...

NASH: Good luck!

SARIAH: TTYL

When I set my phone aside on the table, it hit the surface harder than I'd intended.

"I'm shocked that didn't go well," Lars said, grinning.

"Fuck off. She's having drinks with someone from the front office tonight."

"Who?"

I held back my urge to kick him under the table. "If I knew, I would have said who."

"If she's pretty, those front office fucks will be all over her. That guy Brad in accounting just got divorced, and I heard he's on the prowl."

"The world is coming to an end," I said, shaking my head. "You just used a euphemism correctly."

"What is euphemism?"

"It's a saying. Like *on the prowl.*"

He grinned. "Sheridan taught me that one."

The server brought back the receipt. Lars signed it and put his debit card back in his wallet.

"Ready to go?" he asked.

"Yeah." I slid out of the booth, taking a mental inventory of all the men who worked for the Mavericks.

"What if it's Hickey Ricky?" I asked Lars.

"It might be. If she has a hickey tomorrow, it was probably him."

"This isn't a joke," I snapped. "It's fucking hard for me to pretend like I don't care who she's having drinks with tonight when what I really want to do is break the dick off of whoever it is."

"Tell her who you are."

I opened the restaurant door and stalked outside, not answering Lars until he caught up with me.

"I'm not ready."

"Sheridan has plans tonight. Do you want to

come over and play video games to keep your mind off Sariah's date?"

I stopped walking. "I have a better idea."

"Basketball?"

"No. We're going out. We just need to figure out where Sariah and—let's face it, probably that bag of dicks—Kevin, are going and then we'll just happen to be there, too."

Lars shook his head. "This is a terrible idea."

"Either be a supportive wingman or shut your piehole."

He put his hands up in surrender. "I'll go, because I enjoy proving I am right."

"How can we figure out where she's going, though?"

Rubbing his chin, Lars considered for a few seconds. "I think I might be able to."

"How?"

"Marla in sales owes me a favor, and she's trustworthy. I can ask her to talk to Sariah and see if she can get her to mention it."

"Yes." I held my fist out. "Thanks, man."

He bumped my fist. "It's a bad idea, but I will pick you up after you trash and burn."

"It's crash and burn, dude."

"Are you sure?"

"Yeah, I'm sure."

CHAPTER ELEVEN

Sariah

WITH THE TEAM back in town, it was busy again. Not just because I had to go to the games, but there was an energy in the office that wasn't there when the team was on the road. I imagined it was even worse in the off-season, and I asked Monique about it that night as we sat at a small, local sports bar having drinks.

"What happens in the summer?" I asked, sipping my glass of chardonnay. "When the team is off and there aren't any games and stuff? Isn't it kind of sad and quiet?"

She chuckled. "Well, yes and no. For me, there isn't much to do and I don't work most of the summer. But the sales team busts their butts to sell season tickets for the upcoming season, so you'll be busy."

"I imagine it's harder to do when the guys aren't around to sign things and stuff."

"A lot of the guys live here year-round. Wes is always available, and while some of the guys go home to Russia or wherever, most of them take a vacation but then come back to town."

"Good to know."

She nodded.

"What do you do all summer then? If you're not working?"

Monique's dark eyes were suddenly shrouded, and she stared off at nothing for a few seconds. "Usually Tony and I travel, spend time together."

"Usually?"

"He's asked for a separation."

"Your husband asked for a separation?" I was flabbergasted. "Oh my god. When did this happen?"

"Day before yesterday."

"You okay?"

"No." She blinked furiously, as if trying to keep the tears welling up in her eyes from falling. "He told me he's not attracted to me anymore."

I gaped at her. "What the hell is wrong with him? You're beautiful!"

She smiled faintly, swiping at her eyes. "Thanks. But I've put on some weight, and he basically told me I was too fat for him now."

"You're not fat," I gasped in horror. "Your body is amazing. I would kill to have an ass like yours."

"Oh, he likes the ass just fine. It's the thicker thighs and the stomach that's not flat anymore that turns him off. I used to be an athlete, a runner, and I guess he got used to that body. The one I had when I worked out all day, every day. Before I got a grown-up job." She managed a tiny eye roll, though her heart didn't seem to be in it.

"I'm so sorry," I whispered. I was shocked and disappointed in a man I didn't even know, but mostly I felt terrible for her. What kind of man said something like that? Because she was truly a stunning woman, with cheekbones for days and a smile that lit up the room.

"I'm thirty-seven," she said quietly. "We were talking about getting pregnant this year. And now..." Her voice trailed off and she lifted her hand, motioning to the bartender to bring us two more drinks.

"Are you going to try counseling or anything?" I asked.

She shook her head. "I don't think so. I'm heartbroken and sad, but I'm also furious. Who does his pigeon-toed, bald-headed ass think he is? Because there is *zero* chance I'm going on some kind of diet to win back a man who promised to love me in sickness and in health and all that bullshit. Uh-uh. No way, no how. Fuck that. If I'm not good enough at this weight, he don't deserve me when I'm in better shape."

"Good for you."

"I don't know what I'm going to do going forward, but I know I'm better off without him."

"I'm so sorry." I put my hand on her arm. "We haven't known each other very long, but I'm here for you, even if it's just to listen."

"I appreciate that." She'd just reached for her drink when her eyes lit up. "Well, now, isn't this a fun surprise!"

"What?" I turned in confusion, my gaze landing on…Nash freakin' Reilly.

The amount of heat that man oozed was downright disconcerting. Even in low-slung jeans and a Metallica T-shirt, my lady parts sat right up and took notice, no matter how many times I told them to shut the fuck up. When Monique waved him and Lars Jansson over, I nearly groaned with frustration.

"Hey, Mo." Nash hugged her tightly. "You doin' okay?"

"Hangin' in there." She smiled. "You know Sariah, right?"

"I do." He turned and fixed those damn blue eyes on me, leaving me a little breathless. "How are you?"

"I'm well, thank you." I forced myself not to stare at his broad shoulders or flat stomach, keeping my gaze firmly on his face.

"Do you know Lars?" He turned to his tall, burly teammate. "Lars, this is Sariah, the new woman in sales. Sariah, Lars."

"Hello. I've seen you around, but we haven't formally met."

I shook his hand.

"I have heard many nice things about you," Lars said, his eyes meeting mine as we shook.

"That's good to hear." I smiled.

"You've been selling season tickets like a boss," Monique said, nudging me. "*Everyone* is talking about you."

I grimaced. "Hopefully, not everyone."

We all chuckled.

"Sorry I am late." Another guy from the team, Konstantin Volkov, came up to the bar, standing beside us. He had a thick Russian accent and what I could only describe as a sad smile that didn't reach his eyes.

"Hey!" Michael Boone joined us a few seconds later and Nash motioned to the bartender.

"Hey, man, can we put a few tables together?" he asked.

"Absolutely. I'll send over a waitress."

"Would you two like to join us?" Nash asked, looking at Monique and me.

"Sure." Monique got to her feet and picked up her glass of wine before I could respond, so I had no choice but to follow.

We sat around two high-top tables and a waitress showed up with menus and a couple of pitchers of beer.

"Is Sawyer coming?" Nash asked as we got settled, referring to Sawyer Cain, another one of their teammates.

Lars shook his head. "Annie is very sick. Sheridan just texted me that he's taking her to the hospital."

"Oh, fuck. Not again." Nash shook his head.

"Who's Annie?" I asked.

"Sawyer's wife," Nash said quietly. "She has cancer and it's spread. She was doing well for a while, but she's been in and out of the hospital all winter and spring. I don't think the prognosis is very good."

"Oh, no. That's terrible."

"We try to be there for them," Lars said. "But it is a very difficult situation."

"I can't imagine," Monique said. "Every time I start feeling sorry for myself about my separation, I think of Sawyer and Annie and am grateful for the life I have."

"Wait, you're getting divorced?" Boone asked, clearly irritated by the news. "Do I need to kick Tony's ass?"

"I already tried," Nash said, shaking his head. "But she won't let me."

"You guys are sweet, but it serves no purpose," she said, shrugging. "You can't beat him into loving me again."

"No, but we can beat his ass just for fun." Lars cracked his knuckles, the look on his face so deadly I wasn't sure whether or not he was serious.

"I think I might love you, Lars Jansson." Monique grinned at him and though his face remained impassive, his ears turned red, which I thought was endearing. "But no one beats on him, understand? I plan to do all the damage in court."

"My fiancée has the best divorce lawyer in the state," Lars told her. "If you need her number, let me know."

"Thank you. I'm not quite ready for that, but I'll let you know when I am."

"What about you, Sariah?" Boone asked, looking at me. "You single? Taken?"

"Single," I said. "Got out of a long relationship about six months ago and I'm enjoying my freedom."

"I swear there's something in the air," Monique said, shaking her head. "I know two other couples getting divorced. Kevin from the sales department got divorced last year too."

"My girlfriend also left me last year," Kon said somberly.

"I think we need a shot after this pity fest," Nash said, motioning to the waitress. "Tequila or Jägermeister?"

Monique groaned. "I don't do tequila. That's what got me into this mess. Shots of tequila led to a one-night stand that never left. Nope. I am *never* swallowing another worm."

I snorted and then clapped a hand over my mouth.

"Girl..." Monique gave me a dirty look even as she dissolved into laughter.

"Jägermeister it is!" Nash said firmly, winking at me.

I opened my mouth to protest, because I almost never did shots and had never tried Jägermeister, but I couldn't very well say no when everyone else was doing it. I was having a good time and really liked everyone I'd met. I hadn't expected to ever go out drinking with guys on the team, but now that I was here, it felt natural.

When the waitress brought the round of shots, I wrinkled my nose at the dark liquid, peering at it with distaste.

"You've never done a Jäger shot before, have you?" Nash whispered, leaning toward me.

I gave a slight shake of my head. "No. How bad is it?"

"Licorice," he said in my ear. "If you can tolerate licorice, you'll be okay."

"You're downplaying it. I can tell."

"No. I swear. It's not that bad if you don't mind licorice. Come on, we'll do it together." He scooted his barstool closer, until the side of his thigh was pressed against mine, and lifted his glass. "To making the playoffs."

"To new friends." Monique met my gaze warmly.

"No more breaking up," Kon said firmly.

"Amen to all of the above." Boone brought the shot to his lips.

I squeezed my eyes shut and poured the liquid down my throat. I couldn't help the shudder of horror that escaped me, and I probably made an extremely unattractive face, but it tasted like licorice-flavored death laced with poison.

"Sweet Jesus, why does anyone drink this?" I gasped.

Nash surreptitiously passed me the glass of water he'd ordered when he sat down, and I grabbed it like a lifeline. Normally I wouldn't have drunk from a stranger's glass, but the lingering taste of the liquor was more than I could stand.

"Thank you," I said to him gratefully.

"Of course." The smile he gave me made me temporarily forget the horrible aftertaste in my mouth and I smiled back.

"Not much of a drinker?" he asked.

"Oh, I drink, but I don't do shots very often. Especially ones that taste like that. I'll take tequila over that nonsense any day."

"Agreed. I try to stick to beer, especially during the season, but once in a while you have to let loose and doing a shot for Monique felt appropriate tonight."

"You guys seem close."

"We are. She's a lot of fun and a consummate professional. The clips she makes for me so I can watch video on my own time are exactly what I need and technically she doesn't have to make them of just my plays, you know?"

"She seems like the type to go above and beyond."

"Absolutely."

"Have you met her husband?" I asked under my breath.

He gave a little nod, but there was no mistaking the distaste on his face. "He's an arrogant prick. I've never understood what she sees in him, but it wasn't my place to say that. I'm just extremely pissed off that he's hurt her. She deserves better."

It surprised me that Nash felt so passionately about what Monique's husband had done. I hadn't expected that kind of emotional depth from him, which made me feel a little guilty because I knew firsthand what it was like to be judged on looks alone. Maybe he wasn't so bad.

"I don't even know the guy and I want to throat punch him," I said after a moment.

"Maybe Mo will let you at him since she won't let us do it," he said, loud enough for her to hear.

"Don't you go putting any ideas in her head!" Monique said to him, wagging her finger. "She does *not* need to be corrupted by the Mavericks!"

"I think it's too late for that," Boone said, his dark eyes twinkling. "She's one of us now, so…" His voice trailed off as he shrugged.

"Too late for what?" I asked, looking around the table.

"Oh, you'll see." Nash had an innocent look on his

face but there was no mistaking the laughter brewing beneath the surface.

"Don't listen to them!" Monique called to me. "You just stay your sweet, innocent self. These boys are *not* to be trusted."

"You wound me, Mo!" Nash clasped his chest, as if in pain.

They continued their back-and-forth banter, and despite Monique's playful warning, warmth filled me. It had been a long time since I'd been part of a group that made me feel like I belonged. I hadn't been part of the Mavericks organization very long, but I *was* one of them now, and I liked it.

CHAPTER TWELVE

Nash

"How can you not call that? What the fuck? That was slashing!"

Our entire bench erupted as Lars took a stick to the face. Even Coach was worked up, gesturing and yelling as our offensive lines made a change.

"Somebody get that ref a Chicago jersey!" I yelled.

The fans behind us were also not having it. St. Louis and Chicago had a major hockey rivalry, and every seat in the Chicago arena was full tonight. We needed this win, because the momentum wasn't on our side right now, and I didn't have another grueling bag skate in me.

The crowd roared as a fight broke out between Lars and the guy who had slashed him, McGill. Instinct made me stand up, ready to join the fight, but Wes put his arm out to stop me.

"He doesn't need you," he said, watching the scene a lot more calmly than I was.

Becoming our team captain after Ben died had somehow mellowed Wes. He'd learned in the year and a half he'd been captain to choose his battles, and to be a calming force for our team.

"Un-fucking-believable," I grumbled. "Guess decent vision isn't a requirement to become a ref these days."

"He was looking right at it," Wes said. "That fucking ref is just being an asshole."

The game was tied, each team having two goals as we approached the last minute. When the first line went back in for our shift, my focus was entirely on getting the puck into the net. Wes, Boone, and I passed it back and forth, my heart racing faster than usual.

We were in the playoffs. Last season, after losing Ben and his wife, we'd scraped through and ended the season below five hundred. But this season, our first without Ben, we wanted to win for him. I wanted it more than I'd ever wanted anything. We'd shed many tears together as we moved forward in a daze last year, broken by the loss of our friend and captain.

He and Lauren would never see their two young children grow up. Wes and Lauren's friend, Hadley, were raising them now, with our entire team behind them. Every time I saw Ben's daughter in the family box wearing her Mavericks sweater, her face painted in our team colors, I wanted to win the Cup for her.

I was in perfect scoring position. The Chicago tender was all fucking over me, though, so instead of shooting, I passed it to Boone. He slid it into the net like a pro and the arena erupted in both cheers and groans.

"Attaboy!" I said as Wes, Boone, and I made a circle.

"We might just have the hang of this, boys," Wes said, grinning.

He looked up at the box his family was sitting in and raised his stick. I followed his gaze and barely made out Annalise, who had both arms in the air and a huge smile on her face.

I wondered for a split second whether I'd ever have a family cheering for me up there. I'd always assumed I'd have a family, but it was easy to assume that when you knew it was still a decade or more away. Given what was going on between me and my dad, I wasn't so sure now.

We held off Chicago and won the game with a final score of 3–2. The mood in the locker room was light, with everyone talking about going out.

"You in?" Boone asked me.

"Yep, as long as we go to a place that has real food. I'm starving."

It had been six hours since Lars and I ate our traditional pregame meal, a plateful of pasta, and I was jonesing for a burger. I was talking to some fans at the bar we were eating at, waiting for my food, when I got a text. I smiled, hoping it was from Sariah.

It was from my mom, though.

MOM: Hi Nash, great game tonight! I was cheering for you from our living room. I know you're busy, but call me when you can. I'd really like you to make it to the anniversary party. Love you.

It was unlike her to text me so late. I apologized to the fans at the bar and walked back to our table and sat down, writing her back.

NASH: Hey Mom, thanks. I'll try to make it. Is everything okay? You're not usually up this late.

MOM: I just couldn't fall asleep after the game. It was so exciting. Your dad is out of town for work, and I've become a night owl when I'm on my own.

NASH: Is that a lot?

MOM: A couple nights a week at least. Your dad has been very busy with work lately.

I shook my head, picturing my mom home by herself, lonely. Immediately, it made me feel guilty.

NASH: Why don't you come visit me and the dogs? They miss you. We can go to some of your favorite restaurants.

MOM: I wish I could, honey, but I'm volunteering for the hospice center again. They're really short on help.

NASH: That's nice of you.

MOM: I'm so proud of you. I cried when I saw your face on the TV screen tonight. I really hope you can make it to our anniversary party.

NASH: I'll do my best, Mom. Promise.

MOM: Are you out with your teammates?

NASH: Yes, just waiting on some food.

MOM: Okay, I'll let you get back to them. Be safe and have fun.

NASH: Always. Love you.

I stuck my phone back in my pocket, sighing heavily. Though I really didn't want to, I was going to have to go to the anniversary party. It meant a lot to my mom. I just had to set aside my feelings about my dad.

The glass of water I'd ordered when we got here was half empty. I went to reach for it, but lowered my hand back to the table. I needed a beer. I hadn't planned on drinking tonight so I'd feel fresher for a big workout in the morning, but there was nothing like thinking about my dad to make me change my mind on that.

———

AN HOUR LATER, I was watching Boone try to get a woman to go home with him, and it was nothing if not amusing. There was a one-hundred-percent chance this woman had gotten in here with a fake ID, because she was nowhere close to twenty-one.

"What's your favorite college class?" Boone asked her.

She laughed nervously. "Science. I like the experiments and stuff. It's just so *brainy*, you know?"

"I like science, too," he said. "And I think smart chicks are hot."

Her response was a giggle. I met Boone's gaze and shook my head.

"What's your major?" he asked her.

"I don't know yet, maybe fashion? I'm like, *obsessed* with fashion. I either want to be a model or a social media influencer."

"You could be both," he suggested. "Like the Kardashians."

"Oh my god, I like, *love* the Kardashians. Which one is your favorite? Mine is Kendall Jenner."

Boone shrugged. "I don't know. I guess Kim? She does some cool shit."

The woman wrinkled her nose. "Kim is like, *old*, though."

Jesus. Once upon a time I'd been just like Boone, pretending to care as some vapid woman talked and talked about absolutely nothing.

I'd texted Sariah after the game, but hadn't heard back, so I was surprised when a message from her came through a little after midnight.

SARIAH: I woke up and can't get back to sleep. Are you awake by chance?

This was a nice surprise. I texted back immediately.

NASH: I am. And this is funny, because my mom just texted me a little bit ago that she can't sleep, either.

SARIAH: Weird. I keep looking at the clock thinking about how much sleep I can still get, and then stressing when I still don't fall asleep. Recalculate. Stress again. Repeat.

NASH: Busy day at work tomorrow?

SARIAH: Just the usual. What about you?

NASH: A little busy. It's an early morning, but a short day.

SARIAH: Want me to let you go so you can sleep?

NASH: Nope.

SARIAH: How's your mom? And where does she live, by the way?

NASH: My parents have been in Asheville for several years now. And she's okay. She's alone again tonight because my dad's a worthless asshole.

SARIAH: That's terrible.

NASH: Yeah, and the worst part is, my mom doesn't even know.

I set my phone back on the table and took a sip of my second beer of the night. I'd never told anyone what was up with my parents. Saying it out loud seemed like it would just make it worse. Texting about it didn't seem as bad, though. And Sariah was a good listener. She might have some advice for me about the anniversary party.

SARIAH: Want to tell me about it?

NASH: A couple of years ago, my dad asked me to get him tickets to a hockey game in NY for him and a business associate. I ended up being in town at the last minute, so I went to meet up with him. Thought maybe we could go get a drink. When I got there, he was with a woman and he had his arm around her.

SARIAH: Oh no.

NASH: Yeah. He just introduced her as Sandy like it was no big deal. I left and confronted him about it later and he told me he hasn't been happy with my mom in a long time and he'd started seeing Sandy almost a year earlier. Fucking shitbag.

SARIAH: And he never told your mom?? This whole time??

NASH: No. He said it would break her heart and that he doesn't want to do that to her.

SARIAH: But he already did it to her.

NASH: Believe me, I agree. We went a few rounds about it. And now he's trying to get me to go to their thirtieth anniversary party next month.

SARIAH: Oh, my heart just broke for her. An anniversary party, and she has no idea he's been cheating on her for two years now.

NASH: Yeah, and she's the sweetest person. She doesn't deserve any of this.

SARIAH: What are you going to do?

NASH: Idk. I've thought about telling her, but that's something my dad needs to man up and do himself.

SARIAH: I can't even imagine doing that to another person. Have you ever cheated on someone?

NASH: Never. Either you're happy enough to be faithful, or you break up.

SARIAH: I don't think I could go to that party if I were you.

NASH: I really don't want to, but my mom keeps asking me to come. She wants to introduce me to her friends there. I'm an only child.

SARIAH: That's really hard.

NASH: Yeah, it sucks.

"Hey man, I'm heading out," Wes said, tapping my shoulder.

I looked up and saw that my teammates had started clearing out of the bar while I was busy texting Sariah.

"Yeah, I will too," I said.

NASH: We should both get to bed. Thanks for listening.

SARIAH: Anytime. Good night, Rob.

I felt a stab of guilt over the fake name I'd given her. What the hell was I going to do about all of this? I didn't want to tell her the truth, because she'd be pissed—rightfully so.

Fuck. I sounded exactly like my douchebag father.

NASH: Good night.

CHAPTER THIRTEEN

Sariah

"Hey, Sariah?" Kevin looked up from his desk. "I have Everett Jackson on the phone and he says he wants to talk to you."

"Thanks! Send him my way." I waved at him as he transferred the call and picked it up on the first ring. "Everett!"

"Sara!" Everett Jackson was a retired professional baseball player who now ran a fitness center in St. Louis. I'd sold him tons of ad space when I'd worked for the newspaper and he'd called me Sara from the first time we'd met, no matter how many times I'd corrected him. One night at a charity function, he'd gotten drunk and admitted he did it just to hear me get huffy about it. Now it was our joke.

"You've been a hard man to reach," I told him.

"I had no idea you'd left the paper," he protested. "You didn't call me!"

"You were in Europe for two months and didn't tell me." I pointed out. "You've been on my list of people to call, but I've been swamped since I joined the Mavericks organization. Everyone is buying season tickets."

"You're gonna make me watch hockey now, aren't you?" he groaned. "And Maya is going to divorce me if I add another sport to the list."

"Hockey is awesome!" I said, laughing. "Way more exciting than baseball."

"Hey, now." He chuckled good-naturedly.

"Well, it is, but that's not the point. I actually didn't reach out for season tickets because I know that's not your jam. But I thought you might want to put an ad in one of our game-day programs. Ad space is quite reasonable and—"

"You don't need to hard sell me," he interrupted. "You know I'll advertise anywhere you tell me to. So give me a full page near the back, where the player bios are. We'll start with the first two games of the playoffs. You know where to send the mock-ups and the bill. My assistant will approve or make suggestions, but you know what I like."

"Don't you want to know how much—" I tried again.

He just laughed. "Don't know, don't care. Tax write-off. Talk soon!" He disconnected and I couldn't help but laugh.

Sure, I'd worked hard to make most of my contacts through the paper, but the Mavericks were so hot right now they were practically selling themselves.

"Let me guess," Kevin said, strolling over to my desk. "You sold five thousand more season tickets and now you have a waiting list until the year 2050."

I glanced up at him, surprised at the mocking tone in his voice.

"No, smartass. I sold a full-page ad in the program for a couple of playoff games. What's your problem?" I knew from experience to never let anyone, especially not men, condescend to me or they would all do it and my life would be hell.

"You know how long I've been trying to get a foothold at Jackson Athletics?"

I arched a brow. "Everett and I have been business associates and friends since I worked on my college newspaper. That's an established relationship. I'm sorry you feel like I stepped on your toes, but that's not how it is. I've been to his home, I've met his wife and kids, and he always takes my calls. It had nothing to do with you."

Kevin sighed. "Man, it's always the pretty girls." He shook his head and walked back to his desk, muttering.

"What's always the pretty girls?" A voice whispered behind me, and I started, swinging around to see Nash standing there with a large Starbucks coffee that I had a sneaking suspicion was for me. This would be the third time he'd brought me one in the last two weeks if it was, and I didn't understand why he was hanging around so much.

I shrugged. "He's mad I landed the Jackson Athletics account, but Everett was already my client. I can't help that I brought a lot of my clients with me. And anyway, Everett and his wife are also friends, so he was never going to get that one."

Nash looked over at Kevin and made a face before glancing down at me. "You know that's not what he's really mad about, right?"

"What do you mean?" I looked up as he handed me the coffee. "And thank you—but you don't have to bring me coffee every time you come up here."

"I know, but I want to. And you're welcome." He perched one butt cheek on the edge of my desk and lowered his voice. "Kevin wants to take you out, but since you've made it clear you're not interested in dating anyone you work with, he's acting out the only way he can."

My mouth fell open. "Seriously? What is this, first grade?"

He shrugged. "You asked. I'm telling you what I see."

"I didn't ask, but ugh." I sipped my coffee and tried to muster up some indignation, but the sweet caramel on my tongue made it difficult to be grumpy. "He's old enough to be my dad."

"He also knows you're way out of his league. He'll get over it. You're bringing in a lot of money, both in ticket sales and advertising, so when everyone gets a bonus at the end of the season, he'll be singing your praises."

"I guess." I leaned back in my chair. "So, what are you doing up here? Don't you have to rest up for tonight?"

"It's the last game of the regular season. Most of us starters are going to be taking it easy tonight, letting the younger guys get some experience while we try to avoid injuries and fatigue."

"Makes sense."

"You coming to the game?"

"Of course. In fact, my father and brother-in-law are coming too."

"Nice. You need me to sign anything for them?"

I hesitated. My father would probably get a kick out of a signed puck, but I hated to ask for anything personal.

"I'll send up a couple of signed pucks once I go back downstairs," he said after a moment. "It's no problem."

"Thank you." I was flustered and didn't understand why. It wasn't like there was anything going on between us, but there was something about him, about the way he looked at me sometimes, that made me feel like we had a connection. It was superficial at best, but it existed and denying it would have been stupid.

I kept trying to find fault with him, but despite his bawdy sense of humor and the way he charmed every woman in every room he walked into, there was more to Nash than met the eye.

"Hey, Nash." Lance came over to us, cocking his head. "Do you need anything?"

"I came up to sign some postcards for Sariah and anyone else who needs them," Nash lied smoothly. "With the playoffs coming, I figure I won't have as much time so I thought I'd take care of that now."

I quickly pulled out the stack of postcards I had in my drawer and put them on my desk. "Chop-chop, buddy."

Nash chuckled.

"We appreciate it," Lance said. He turned and looked around, letting out a low whistle. "Hey! All-hands meeting in ten minutes. Conference Room A."

I grimaced, wondering what that could be about since we'd never had an all-hands meeting in the five weeks I'd been here.

"I'll sign a few dozen of these," Nash murmured. "Get back to work."

I kicked his foot with mine. "Sure, now that you almost got me into trouble."

He winked and snatched the black Sharpie from my hand.

THE MEETING TURNED out to be about Nash, which was kind of funny. He'd been getting so much fan mail since the underwear ad had come out, the media relations department and their interns simply couldn't keep up. Though much of it was filled with the usual excitement, the team felt strongly about having a person look at every single letter. They didn't want to miss anything important, like a request from a sick child or something like that. Nash had initially said he would pay for the postage so that every single person who wrote to him would get an autographed postcard, but there were over ten thousand pieces of mail now. It had gotten unwieldy, so the higher-ups had asked that everyone who worked in the executive offices take a few minutes every day to help out.

Even if it was only ten minutes, if everyone did it, we might be able to keep up. So Monique and I ordered takeout for lunch and used one of the small conference rooms to eat, go through fan mail, and chitchat.

"I feel like you're holding out on me," she said, once our food had arrived and we shut the door behind us.

"Holding out?" I frowned. "What are you talking about?"

"Don't even try to pretend there isn't a little somethin' somethin' going on with you and Nash." Her eyes twinkled with delight even as I shook my head vigorously.

"Are you kidding me? Of course there isn't anything going on with us!" I stared at her. "How unprofessional would that be?"

She arched her perfectly shaped brows in disbelief. "Unprofessional? Girl, if I was a decade younger and single like you, I'd be all over his fine ass!"

"No, you wouldn't." I pointed to the open letter in front of me. "Have you read some of this nonsense?

These women are hard core. I can't imagine being his girlfriend or anything else with the kind of attention he gets. This is the kind of thing that makes relationships a nightmare."

"This…" She motioned to the box of letters on the table. "Is mostly make believe. Women with fantasies who are never, ever going to even breathe the same air as him. Nash, on the other hand, is a living, breathing human being with feelings and a heart and a good head on his shoulders. He knows the difference between crazy fans and someone he could build a future with."

"Now you're the one who's dreaming," I responded. "Besides, there's kind of someone in my life already."

Monique gaped at me. "You've been seeing someone and didn't tell me?"

"Kinda?" I scrunched up my nose, trying to decide how to explain my relationship with Rob. "His name is Rob." I told her how I'd accidentally texted him and everything that had happened since then.

"Talk about make believe." She leaned forward, her face more serious now. "Listen, I get that you've been careful with this guy, not giving him your full name or where you work or anything, but why would you ignore something with real potential for someone who might be a faux European prince just waiting for your bank card number?"

"I've talked to him on the phone, so he's almost definitely American. He might be a fifty-year-old dude living in his grandmother's basement, but he's no weird prince or anything."

"But you obviously have reservations or you would have met him in person already."

I chewed the inside of my cheek, because she was right. I did have reservations. Rob could be anyone, of any age or background, and that was intimidating. "I do worry about who he really is, but at the same time, he's someone I think I'd want to go out with at some point. Assuming everything he's told me is true."

"And what if he's exactly who he says he is, except really unattractive?"

"Believe me, I've thought of all these things. He's just so easy to talk to. We have a lot in common. He's down-to-earth, a really good listener, and he loves animals. He has a busy career like I do and—"

"That could be a lie."

I opened another letter. "Look, you're not telling me anything I haven't already considered. I'm just not sure what to do about it yet."

"Promise me if you decide to meet him in person,

you'll tell me when and where so I can be there for backup." Her dark eyes gleamed with intensity.

"I promise."

She patted my hand, temporarily mollified. "Meanwhile, let's talk about these coffee breaks you keep taking with Nash."

CHAPTER FOURTEEN

Nash

"Are you kidding me?"

Eric Alvarado pulled a block of ice from his locker and glared at me.

"Why is there ice in your locker?" I asked, feigning innocence.

"It's because you have the intellect of an eight-year-old," he grumbled, setting the ice down on the bench.

"Pop that sucker under a hot shower and you'll have your jock on in no time for practice," Wes said, clapping him on the shoulder. "It'll be wet, though."

Alvarado balked. "My jock is in that thing?"

"Yeah, dipshit," Drew said. "Did you think it was just a big chunk of ice?"

Yesterday, I'd had to dump a bag of ice out of the front office's employee break room freezer to make room for a bucketful of water with Alvarado's compression shorts in the middle, and now it was frozen solid.

"What the fuck am I supposed to do?" Alvarado asked. "I need my jock for practice."

I gave him a serious look. "Don't worry, we won't deliberately shoot pucks at your crotch. We promise."

A snicker sounded from a few lockers away.

"You're an asshole," Alvarado said, pointing at me and then picking up the block of ice. "I'll wear it wet."

He turned and stormed toward the showers. Wes grinned at me and spoke in a hushed tone.

"I assume there's Icy Hot in it, too?"

"You know it."

He set his roll of tape down on the bench. "Any reason you're hitting him so hard?"

I shrugged. "Because he's being such a douchebag about it."

"Is everyone dressed in here?" a female voice yelled into the locker room.

We all looked over to see that the door to the

locker room was cracked open, but no one was walking in.

"Everyone but Boone, but it takes a powerful magnifying glass to see his junk!" I answered.

The voice laughed. "Seriously, is everyone dressed? I need to come in."

Lars walked over and opened the door, dressed only in his jock and leggings. "We are all dressed. Come on in."

"Oh." Sariah walked in, averting her eyes from Lars's bare chest.

Her gaze immediately landed on my bare chest, and she looked down at the floor. Her cheeks were tinted pink with embarrassment.

"We've all got pants on," I assured her.

"That's good, it's just…I'm used to seeing you guys with shirts on, too."

"You'll get used to it," Wes said. "Most of us usually don't have shirts on in here."

"I'm sorry to barge in," she continued. "But I need this jersey signed by as many players as I can get so I can close a sale on a VIP box, and I figured it would be easier for me to come to you guys than to ask you all to stop by the front office."

"We appreciate that," Wes said, taking a Sharpie and the jersey from her. "You want it personalized?"

"No, just your signatures would be great."

"Who's the big dog buying the VIP box?" I asked her.

"It's a friend of Rosa Romano's. I asked her if she had any leads for me, and she had several."

Rosa Romano was our team owner. She and her late husband had made a fortune together, and she liked people with initiative. I was betting she liked Sariah a lot.

Everyone passed the jersey around for signatures, and then Sariah checked the list on her clipboard.

"I'm just missing Eric Alvarado. Is he here today?"

"He's occupied, but I'll take it to him real quick," Wes offered.

"Thanks."

I sat down to put my skates on and looked up at Sariah. "You keep going at the pace you're setting and before long we'll need a new arena with more seating."

"That would be a good problem to have." She smiled and tucked a lock of hair behind her ear. "I feel like I should have brought you a coffee. This is like your office, right?"

"My office is the last stall in the bathroom," I quipped. "But you definitely don't want to bring me coffee in there."

"Do you guys drink coffee?"

"Some of us do."

Drew made a face. "Not me, dude. Coffee gives me the shits."

"Yeah, because you drink like five cups at a time," I said.

I looked at Sariah again. "It's a big problem for a goalie to have the shits because he can't leave the ice."

"Oh, god. That's…"

I laughed. "You're getting an up close and personal look at hockey today."

Wes brought the jersey back, and Alvarado was right behind him, giving me a pissed-off glare.

"Are things a little moist in there, Alvie?" I asked him.

"Don't call me that."

"The rookie has a nickname!" Drew called to everyone. "Alvie!"

"You guys are a bunch of assholes," Eric muttered.

"Hey, there's a lady in the room," I said.

"Who, you?" he scoffed. "You're almost as pretty as she is."

He reached down and adjusted himself and immediately made a face. "Holy shit, what the…?"

Grabbing his crotch, he turned and ran toward the bathroom, pulling his pants down on the way.

"Is he okay?" Sariah asked, looking concerned.

"He will be. Just got a nice big shot of Icy Hot on his balls."

Her mouth dropped open in shocked amusement.

"The rookies are the butt of pranks around here," I said.

Laughing, she said, "I'll leave you guys to it. Thanks for the signatures."

She left the locker room and I finished putting my skates on, then checked my phone one last time before practice. I saw a text from Sariah that had been sent around thirty minutes ago.

SARIAH: Just thinking about you. How's your day going?

NASH: Better now that I've heard from you. How's your day?

I figured she left her phone on her desk, but she must have had it in her pocket because she wrote back immediately.

SARIAH: I'm close to closing a big sale. I think I might be pretty good at this job.

NASH: Of course you are. Whoever you work for, they're lucky to have you.

SARIAH: I've been thinking about what you said about us meeting. I'm not ready to meet tonight or anything, but I was thinking...soon?

Shit. I couldn't meet her as Rob, but I also didn't want to blow her off and hurt her feelings. The hole this lie had me in just kept getting deeper.

NASH: I'm leaving tomorrow for a work trip, but maybe after that?

SARIAH: Yes. What will we do for our first meeting?

NASH: Well, according to the conditions of my parole, I can't leave the city or be out after dark.

I waited for a response, but after about a minute, I couldn't hold out any longer.

NASH: Completely joking! My rap sheet consists of one speeding ticket, which was total BS.

SARIAH: Ha! You had me there for a second.

NASH: What can I say? I love a good joke.

SARIAH: I just found out a guy who works at the same place I do played a funny prank on a coworker today.

Ding ding ding. Sariah was talking about me to Rob. I just hoped this time she wouldn't make fun of my one and only foray into modeling.

NASH: Yeah? What was it?

SARIAH: Icy Hot in his underwear, I think?

NASH: Savage. I like this guy.

SARIAH: He keeps the mood light.

NASH: What would you like to do the first time we meet?

SARIAH: What would I like to do? Do you mean like...?

NASH: I mean a detailed list of sex acts, obviously. What did you think I meant?

SARIAH: Okay, this time I know you're joking.

NASH: ;)

SARIAH: Dinner?

NASH: What's your favorite restaurant in the Lou?

SARIAH: I'm not picky. I like small locally owned places.

NASH: Perfect. I know of a great little Italian place.

SARIAH: BREADSTICKS <3

"Hey Nash!" Wes yelled from the door to the locker room. "You coming to practice today?"

I looked up and saw that the locker room had emptied while I was immersed in my text exchange with Sariah.

"Yeah, on my way."

NASH: GTG, duty calls!

SARIAH: Better than doodie calling, right?

NASH: Ba dum bum! I feel like you've been saving that one.

SARIAH: Possibly...

NASH: Text later?

SARIAH: Sure.

I put my phone back in my locker and grabbed

the gear I needed for practice. As expected, I was the last player on the ice.

"Nice of you to join us, Reilly," Coach said.

"Sorry, Coach."

He wasn't really mad. How could he be? We were in the playoffs. Practices these days were light and easy, mostly just some skating and a few shooting drills. We had to save our energy for game nights.

It was during one of our shooting drills that Alvarado bypassed the net and fired a puck directly at me instead. It hit me in the thigh, but I hardly felt it with my pads on.

"What the hell was that, Alvarado?" Coach yelled.

"He's just a lousy shot, Coach," I said.

Shaking his head, Alvarado said, "My hand slipped."

"I heard you've got wet drawers on today," Coach said, grinning.

"I do, Coach. Thanks to Reilly."

"Everyone was a rookie once, Alvarado," Coach said. "Take your lumps."

Practice was so casual today that we had time for conversations while we were skating. Lars skated up next to me and said, "Hey."

"Hey, man."

"Are you going to ask Sariah out?"

I shrugged. "I think it's too soon."

"Why?" He scrunched his face in confusion.

"I can just tell she's not going to be into that. It needs to happen organically."

"Organically?"

"Yeah, like the other night when we were all out. Next time I'll offer her a ride home. One thing can lead to another…"

"And it won't seem at all suspicious to her that you just happen to know where she is yet again?"

"It'll be fine. She's warming up to me."

He grunted. "She won't be so warm when she finds out you've been scamming her."

I looked over both shoulders to make sure no one had overheard him.

"Don't say shit like that when people are around," I hissed. "No one knows but me and you, asshole. And I'm not scamming her."

"Lying to her is better?"

"I'm working on it, okay? I just don't want to ruin everything."

He was about to respond when we had to make an abrupt stop behind Alvarado, who had stopped skating and was bent over at the waist.

"Fuck," Alvarado muttered.

"Are you okay?" Lars asked.

Alvarado put out a hand. "I'm fine. Leave me alone."

He leaned back up and took off on his skates, flying toward the chute.

"Where the hell are you going?" Coach yelled.

"Bathroom!"

"I wonder if he has that stomach flu that's going around," Boone said, stopping beside me and Lars.

"He might," Lars said. "The doorman at our building has been very sick with it."

"Nah, I don't think it's serious," I said.

Lars scoffed. "Are you a doctor now? How would you know?"

"I'm not a doctor, but if I wanted to play one on TV, I think I'd do pretty great." I cleared my throat. "Get me a CBC, chem panel, and a pelvic exam, stat."

Boone laughed. "You're such a dumbass."

Lars's brows were lowered in a serious expression. "I think I will just grab my bag after practice and go. I don't want that flu. Sheridan stopped her birth control and she could get pregnant anytime, and I don't want to get her sick."

"Yeah?" I clapped him on the shoulder. "That's fucking awesome, dude."

"Not if I get her sick with the flu."

"Don't worry about that." I waved a hand. "Alvarado doesn't have the flu. I put laxatives in his water bottle."

Boone roared with laughter. "Oh damn, I wish I could be in that locker room right now."

"We may not be able to see him, but we can listen to it later," I said. "I put an audio recorder in the bathroom."

Arching his brows in amusement, Boone said, "Remind me never to get on your bad side, bro."

CHAPTER FIFTEEN

Sariah

I'D STARTED PACKING for the big move to my new apartment and I was exhausted. It was actually a relief to go to work. My goal was to pack one box each night after work and then pack as many as possible on my days off. I also found myself sorting through stuff I didn't need anymore, which made the packing process take even longer. I took perverse pleasure in throwing out things that had been Theo's, like a can of shaving cream in the back of the bathroom cabinet and an entire box of his daily contact lenses. There were also books, magazines, and a ton of knickknacks I hadn't even noticed until I'd started packing.

I'd signed the lease on my new apartment, and though it was small and had fewer amenities, it was going to make my bank account much happier. One of my goals was to be able to hire a cleaning service once I got settled. With the schedule I worked, I rarely had full days off to catch up on cooking, cleaning, and doing laundry.

When I got into the office on Monday, after packing and purging the day before, I was sore. I'd stopped at Starbucks on the way to work, but this was the kind of day where I secretly hoped Nash would show up with a coffee for me after practice. I was going to need all the caffeine I could get my hands on in the coming weeks.

My phone was ringing as I sat down at my desk and I grabbed it absently. "Sales department. This is Sariah. How may I help you?"

"Hey, it's Mo."

"Hey, girl!"

"There are two huge bags of fan letters in my office that need some love and attention. You wanna come to my office and go through some with me? I need to tell you the latest about Tony and this gives us an excuse to hang out and talk."

"Sure. Give me a few minutes."

"See ya."

I disconnected and took care of some emails that

needed my attention. I'd just gotten up to head to Mo's office when I noticed a familiar pair of blue eyes peering at me from across the room.

Nash.

Holding coffee.

"Hey, Nash." I smiled at him.

"Hi. How was your weekend?" He held out the cup of coffee and I took it.

"Thank you. You have no idea how much I appreciate this. I'm getting ready to move so I spent most of the weekend cleaning and packing. I'm going to need to mainline caffeine the next few weeks."

"I'm happy to contribute to your addiction. Moving is a drag. I don't know your timetable, but if you need any help, I could probably round up a few of the guys."

"Thank you," I said, surprised at the offer. "But I've already hired movers. I don't have a whole lot so it shouldn't be too bad and I'm planning to move personal items and clothes over myself as soon as I get the keys."

"Where are you moving?"

I told him about the small apartment complex about twenty minutes from the arena where I'd found the place I liked.

"The only thing I'm going to miss about my apartment now is the soaker tub and humongous master bathroom. I'm not home enough to care about the other stuff."

"Assuming we're not playing or traveling, let me know the date just in case."

"The fourth."

His lips turned down. "We don't know our schedule that far out. I can't commit to anything."

"It's fine," I said lightly. "You have enough to think about with the playoffs. You don't need to worry about me. Like I said, I hired movers. Anyway, I need to go find Mo."

"Okay." He paused, watching me for a moment, as if there was something on his mind.

"I'll see you later," I said, giving him a little wave.

"Hey, a bunch of us are going to dinner tonight. Why don't you and Mo meet us there?"

I shook my head. "I have to pack. Maybe next time. See you later."

Then I hurried down the hall to Mo's office, as if I needed to get away from the charge of electricity in the air whenever he stood too close to me. I didn't understand it because I didn't even like him. Well, not like *that*. He was a nice enough guy. Just not the guy for me.

He was hot, though. I couldn't deny that.

I shut the door behind me and sank into a chair across from Mo.

"Why do you look flushed?" she asked, frowning at me.

"Huh?" I frowned back, feigning innocence.

"Your cheeks are a little red. You been drooling over Nash again?"

"I don't drool over Nash. He's not even a little bit my type."

"You keep tellin' yourself that."

"He's not! I told you, guys that good-looking come with the type of baggage I don't need in my life."

"You realize that might be the dumbest thing any woman has ever said?"

We glared at each other.

"You're a pain in my ass. You know that?"

"I do. And that's why you love me."

"Tell me about Tony already."

She made a face. "He says he might be willing to go to therapy and maybe we could start working out together. And oh, by the way, he met that hussy he's been seein' on the side at the same gym where he wants us to start working out."

"I hope you told him to go kick rocks."

"I used much stronger language than that."

I laughed. "Good for you."

"I told him we were done. That I was filing for divorce." She hesitated. "Am I making a mistake?"

"He cheated and told you he thinks you're fat," I said quietly. "I don't know how you would ever trust him again. On either count."

"That's what I'm thinking." She pulled out a stack of envelopes and dropped them on the table. "So here we are, reading Nash's fan mail while I contemplate divorce and you crush on some dude popping gummies in his mom's basement."

I rolled my eyes.

———

I WAS home by six that night. The phones had been quiet, there was no game tonight, and it was nice to relax in the tub with a glass of wine after packing a few more boxes. My new place had a decent-sized walk-in shower, but no bathtub, so my days of this kind of relaxation were coming to an end.

I closed my eyes and leaned back, hoping the next few weeks would pass quickly. I was moving in three weeks, which was the middle of the playoffs, and I was stressing. A lot. Luckily, a friend of Sebastian's ran a small moving company, and they were giving me a good deal on moving. I planned to fill my car with clothes and personal items after work every night after I got the keys, so I could make a dent in what had to be brought on moving day. That would save time and money, something I'd been thinking about a lot more lately.

I'd also been thinking about Rob more and more. I was nervous about biting the bullet and meeting him in person, but I liked him. While I was afraid of who he might be in real life, I was also beginning to realize that I was falling for a guy who, in my reality, didn't exist. Wouldn't it be better to meet him and get it over with instead of drawing this out indefinitely?

Picking up my phone, I texted him.

SARIAH: Hey, whatcha doin'?

ROB: Out to dinner with a couple of guys from work.

SARIAH: Oh, okay. I'll leave you alone.

ROB: That's okay. We're at a sports bar and everyone is watching baseball. You don't work for the Cardinals, do you?

SARIAH: No. LOL.

ROB: Are you ever going to tell me where you work?

SARIAH: Eventually.

ROB: Before we both die?

SARIAH: I think we'll be okay.

ROB: What are you up to? More packing?

SARIAH: Already did that. I'm in the tub now.

ROB: That seems to be a thing with us, talking while you're in the tub. Is that a hint that you'd like taking a bath together?

My cheeks warmed just thinking about it.

SARIAH: If we were in a relationship, then absolutely. It just won't be at my new apartment because it doesn't have a tub.

ROB: My place has a MASSIVE tub.

SARIAH: Now you're teasing me.

ROB: Oh, baby, if I was teasing you, you'd know it.

SARIAH: Somehow, I believe that. Hang on a second.

I took the opportunity to get out of the bath, dry off, and wrap myself in a fluffy robe. I padded into the bedroom and stretched out on the bed, looking forward to a nice chat with Rob. I didn't know what to do about him but I was warming up to the idea of us meeting. He seemed so genuine, and my gut rarely steered me wrong. I'd known something was wrong between Theo and me for months, but I'd ignored it because I'd thought the life we had planned was exactly what I wanted. With Rob, the only warning bells that went off were the normal ones related to being careful in a digital world where it was easy to pretend to be someone else. It just didn't feel like he was anything but what he said he was.

SARIAH: I'm back.

ROB: I'm eating wings, so if there's a delay between responses it's because I'm trying to not cover my phone in BBQ sauce.

SARIAH: OK.

ROB: Did I tell you my mom called and really laid the guilt on thick about the anniversary party?

SARIAH: Ugh. What are you going to do? Are you going?

ROB: I don't know how I can NOT go, you know?

SARIAH: But can you go and NOT out your dad?

ROB: That's the problem.

SARIAH: If we get to a point where we've met in person by then, I could go with you. Keep you focused on your mom instead of your anger at your dad.

There was an extra-long pause before he responded, almost making me regret my offer.

ROB: You'd do that? Come with me?

SARIAH: If you wanted me to. If you thought it would help. I can't imagine being in your situation, knowing something so damaging to your parents' relationship and having to keep it a secret.

ROB: It's been tough. It's so fucking stressful.

SARIAH: When is the party?

ROB: Three weeks from this weekend.

SARIAH: That sounds doable. Maybe then you can come with me to my sister's engagement party.

There was another long pause and I nearly held my breath.

What was I doing?

This thing between us still wasn't real. We hadn't

exchanged last names or even told each other where we worked. We hadn't met. I didn't know for sure he was who he said he was, yet here we were making real-life plans. This was either going to be really great or the whole thing was going to blow up in my face.

ROB: This is a conversation for the phone, when I'm not at a bar surrounded by my coworkers.

SARIAH: You're right. Let's table this for now. I need to get some sleep anyway.

ROB: Talk soon, Sariah.

SARIAH: Good night, Rob.

I sighed long and hard as I put my phone down. What had I just done?

CHAPTER SIXTEEN

Nash

"WHAT THE HELL WAS HE THINKING?"

I put my head in my hands and groaned. Beside me on a bench in the locker room, Drew shook his head.

"I don't know, man. But we don't know anything yet. Let's try to keep cool until we hear from him."

Boone laughed, but he was anything but amused. "I'm about as cool as a whore in church, bro. If Wes goes on IR, we are fucked."

He was talking about the injured reserve list. Yesterday afternoon, Wes was trying to get a Frisbee off the roof for Annalise and had fallen as he was climbing down the ladder. His ankle had swollen immediately, but being in complete and total denial that it was a serious injury, he had just iced it and kept it elevated all evening. When he'd woken up this morning, the swelling was worse, so he'd called our team doctor and they'd met up at the hospital. We were all sitting in the locker room waiting for news.

My phone buzzed with a text and I looked down at the screen.

DAD: Your mother needs to get final numbers to our caterer. Will you be at the anniversary party, and will you be bringing a date?

If I could Hulk out, I would've gone big green monster and crushed my phone right there and then. I'd told both of my parents several times that I couldn't commit yet, but that didn't stop my father from pressuring me about it. Part of me wanted to ignore him, but a bigger part wanted to take out my bad mood on him.

NASH: My team is in the playoffs. I don't know if I'll have a game that day, so if you need a yes or a no right now, it's a no.

DAD: Obviously we don't expect you to miss a playoff game for it. But if you don't have a game that day, will you be there?

"Fucking fucker," I muttered at my phone.

"Sariah?" Lars asked from beside me.

I glared at him. "You really think I'd call her that?"

"The chick from sales?" Drew asked me. "Why are you texting her?"

"It's not her." I exhaled hard, feeling frustrated. "The next one of you fuckers who talks to me is getting punched in the face."

I texted my dad back.

NASH: Hey, thanks for your interest in seeing your son's playoff games. I don't know if I can make it to the party to celebrate the marriage you aren't faithful to. I'll let you know.

DAD: Nash, I would love to see your playoff games. If you can arrange for tickets, I'll be there.

NASH: With mom, or with your girlfriend? Or should I get three tickets so you can bring both of them?

DAD: Don't be a smartass. Things are more complicated than you realize.

NASH: It's not complicated to tell Mom you've been cheating on her for two years. She deserves to know.

DAD: I plan to tell her, when the time is right.

Coach Gizzard opened the door to his office and entered the locker room. The room fell silent and I set my phone down on the bench.

"Nothing's broken," he said. "We're going to see how he does over the next week or so with ice and rest, and as of now, we're hopeful he'll be ready for game one."

There was a collective sigh of relief.

Coach looked around the room, stopping on each one of our faces and making eye contact. "There better not be a single word of this spoken outside of this locker room. If I hear of anyone's wife or girlfriend, or even your dear old granny, getting wind of what's going on with Wes, I will put my entire foot up the ass of whoever did it. Clear?"

Everyone answered in agreement, and he went back into his office. If I was Coach, I'd have to pop a Xanax with a shot of whiskey on the daily. There was too much on the line right now for Wes to be climbing a fucking ladder, and he knew it.

"What a stupid shit," Alvarado said to someone a few lockers down from mine. "And he's our captain."

I was full of pent-up anger and frustration—about Wes, about my douchebag father, and about how I was going to get out of the mess I'd gotten myself into with Sariah. Alvarado's dumbass comment caught my attention though, and I channeled all my anger in his direction.

"Say that again, you little cocksucker." I jumped up from the bench and shoved him against his locker.

Alvarado's eyes narrowed with fury as he tried to

push back. I was too fired up, though, and his back slammed into his locker with the force of my next shove, causing him to lose his footing.

"He's not worth getting in trouble over," Lars said from behind me. I felt his hand on my shoulder, his grip firm, and I knew he'd haul me away if I pushed things further.

"What the fuck is your problem?" Alvarado yelled, pushing to his feet.

Boone and Drew crowded around us, ready to intervene if necessary.

"You don't say shit about Wes," I yelled to Alvarado. "He's ten times the player and man you'll ever be. You just got here five minutes ago. Who the fuck do you think you are calling your captain a stupid shit?"

Drew and Boone turned their heads toward Alvarado in an instant, both of them scowling.

"You said that?" Drew demanded.

"I didn't mean—"

Drew punched him right in the gut, and Alvarado doubled over in pain. Throwing his hands in the air, Drew stalked away.

"Do whatever you want to him, Nash," he said dismissively.

Alvarado took a couple seconds to catch his

breath, and I tried to shake off Lars's grip, but he held firm.

"It won't work," he said.

"Fuckin' punk," I said to Alvarado. "No wonder your last team dumped your ass on us."

That got to him. Boone had already turned to go back to his locker and Alvarado took a step toward me.

"If you come closer, I let go of him," Lars said. "You will not like that, Eric."

Alvarado ignored Lars's warning and kept advancing. True to his word, Lars released his hold on me. I ducked the punch Alvarado tried to land and threw a left uppercut at his gut. A right hook to his jaw followed immediately.

He rebounded quickly, ready for more, but Coach's roar stopped both of us cold.

"What the fuck is this?" he demanded.

"He talked shit about Wes," I explained.

"I don't care if he talked shit about your mother. There's no goddamn fighting in this goddamn locker room! Do you dipshits think we need anyone else getting injured?"

"No, Coach," I answered, not even a little bit sorry.

"No, Coach," Alvarado echoed.

"Laps. Both of you." Coach pointed a finger in the

direction of the rink, as if we could see it through the locker room. "If I walk onto that ice, whether it's in half an hour or three hours, and either of you isn't skating, you'll wish you were suspended."

Alvarado shook his head and let out a disgusted sound. Big mistake. Coach was on him before he took his next breath, his face just inches away from Alvarado's.

"You got something to say, rookie? You want to run that big fucking mouth of yours some more?"

Alvarado sobered, shaking his head. "No, Coach."

"You are your own worst goddamn enemy, Alvarado. Keep talking shit about your captain and you'll have a different logo on your chest real quick like."

I was almost done lacing my skates back up. Coach Gizzard didn't lose his shit often, but when he did, most of us knew not to even look at him the wrong way. Everyone was stressed about Wes. Today was not the day to push Coach, even a little.

Alvarado and I skated our laps, maintaining as much distance as possible. Every trip around the rink gave me time to think about Sariah and my parents. I switched back and forth between them, unable to find a solution for either. I was a hamster on a wheel.

"Rob" could ghost Sariah, but I'd need a new

phone number for that to even work. It wasn't the best option, but I couldn't figure out a way to tell her that Nash and Rob were one and the same without making her think I was a manipulator and a liar.

Somehow, I had to end this charade. And while the truth would do the trick, it would also cost me any chance I had of dating her.

Why had I let this get so out of hand? I really liked her, and the truth—the real truth—was that Nash and Rob were both a part of me. The fact that she seemed to like down-to-earth, average Rob more than famous Nash said a lot about who she was.

And my parents? Hell. There was no clean way out of that mess, either. But like Sariah, my mom was in the dark, and it wasn't fair. I wanted to be man enough to make things right with both of them without hurting them in the process.

But how?

After about an hour of skating laps, Coach came and gave us a stern warning, and I went back into the locker room, gassed and not in the mood to do anything but shower, again, and go home to chill with my dogs. When I stepped out of the shower, though, Drew had just finished lifting weights and was waiting for me.

"Hey, you want to get lunch?" he asked.

"Yeah, if it's quick."

"The quicker the better. I'm fucking starving."

"Yeah, let's do it."

He lowered his brows and gave me a puzzled look. "Hey, what did Lars mean about Sariah in sales? Are you seeing her?"

I looked over both shoulders, making sure no one was within earshot. Then I explained the Rob/Nash situation to Drew. He was a longtime teammate and I trusted him. He was also a little older than most of the guys on the team, and good at giving advice.

"Shit, man," he said after hearing the whole story. "You're in a bind."

"Tell me about it. I don't know what to do."

He seemed to be considering my situation as he put on deodorant. "You'll have to come clean at some point, right?"

I nodded. "I want to. But her last boyfriend was dishonest, and—"

"Boyfriend?" His brows shot up in surprise. "You want a relationship with her?"

"Yeah," I said, knowing that I meant it one hundred percent. "I really like her. She's not about the superficial stuff, you know? Talking to her is like talking to a good friend who happens to be sexy as hell. She's smart and funny."

"Dude, that door over there is smarter than your

usual women. I'm really glad to see you interested in a woman with some substance. I haven't been around her much, but she seems great."

"She is. I just have to figure out how to tell her I'm Rob."

Drew laughed. "Man, only you would end up in a situation like this."

"It's not funny. I can't sleep at night because I'm so worried about it."

He clapped me on the shoulder. "We'll talk it over some more at lunch."

We finished dressing and headed for the locker room exit. I checked my phone on the way out and saw a new text from Sariah to Rob.

SARIAH: I have a confession to make. I really like you. It's scary and I'm afraid of getting hurt again and the timing isn't the greatest but...yeah. I like you. And I'm ready for us to meet.

CHAPTER SEVENTEEN

Sariah

IT HAD BEEN MORE than forty-eight hours since I'd texted Rob and told him I wanted to meet, and I hadn't heard a word. Not a text, phone call, smoke signal, or anything else. Just the worst kind of incredibly loud silence. It kind of hurt, but at the same time, it was a relief to know it wasn't going to happen. He probably was probably some forty-year-old dude in his mom's basement after all, and Mo and I would be laughing about it in a few weeks. Or whenever the sting of betrayal eased up. Right now, it felt shitty to have been used even though, technically, he hadn't used me for anything but conversation and friendship.

I kept trying to give him the benefit of the doubt. Maybe he was traveling. Busy in work meetings. Dealing with the situation with his dad. But all of those things had been happening the entire time we'd been talking, and he'd never gone this long without responding to a text. Especially such an important one.

"Girl, who kicked your puppy?" Mo asked, perching on the edge of my desk.

"Huh?" I looked up, realizing I'd been lost in thought.

"You've been in a funk since yesterday. What's wrong with you?"

"Nothing. Just stressed about the move and all that."

"I'm sorry this is happening at the beginning of the playoffs and I'm going to be too busy to help for a bit," she said, giving me a sad look.

"Oh, don't worry about it. My brother-in-law and my younger sister's fiancé have been roped into helping, along with my younger sister. My parents never volunteer but I know damn well Mom is going to insist on unpacking the kitchen and Dad will make a big deal out of setting up my flat-screen TV and stuff. And honestly, as long as my bed, the bathroom, and at least part of the kitchen are set up, everything else can wait. I can do it in the off-season when I'm not working as hard."

"Well, a whole bunch of us are going out tonight and I think you need to come."

I hesitated. "I still have so much to do, Mo."

"I know, but you've been working like a maniac since you started here and you almost never do anything fun. I say we let our hair down for one night. I think both of us deserve it."

"Let our hair down how?" I asked suspiciously.

She shrugged playfully. "I dunno. Shake our booties. Find a couple of cuties to hook up with. A good orgasm is the best way I know to relax."

I laughed. "I can do that on my own. My buddy BOB takes excellent care of me."

"BOB can't go down on you," she murmured. "Or kiss you. Or make your knees weak."

"Those aren't the same as orgasms," I murmured, realizing how long it had been since anyone had done any of those things to me. My sex life with Theo had been a little bland, but up until I figured out he was cheating, there had been intimacy. Cuddling. Kissing. Human contact. I'd never been the type to sleep around, but a one-night stand sounded good right about now.

I was sad and disappointed that Rob had ghosted me, so maybe a casual hookup was just what the doctor ordered. Anything to keep my mind off of him and to keep me from drooling over Nash. I had a history with guys like him. When I'd been doing pageants and modeling, I was surrounded by all the beautiful people and a huge majority had been self-absorbed, petty, and two-faced. The ones I'd dated had been absolute nightmares and I'd vowed to never, ever date someone like that again.

So while on the outside Nash appeared to be everything I didn't want in a man, he was breath-taking to look at and had shown me nothing but kindness since we'd met. The fact that we were friends made it even harder to ignore the growing attraction between us. My brain kept saying I wasn't interested, but now that Rob was probably out of the picture, my body had other ideas.

"You just had the most wicked gleam in your eyes," Mo said, watching me intently.

"Oooh." Nash seemed to appear out of nowhere, making me jump as he leaned against the other corner of my desk. "What wicked thoughts are we having?"

"I'm trying to get Miss Works Too Much to go out with us tonight."

Us?!

She hadn't said a word about Nash joining us.

"No one should work too much," Nash said. "So

you definitely should come out with us. This is probably our last hurrah until the season is over. Coach is going to keep us on a short leash going forward."

"Oh, I don't think—"

"Come on," Nash interrupted me, his eyes meeting mine. They were so damn blue. Like liquid sapphire mixed with passion.

Oh, what the hell was I thinking?

"It'll be fun," Mo said. "And with Nash there, he'll deter any creepers who come sniffing around."

"Well, in that case, I'm in. But you two have to let me get some work done." I made a shooing motion with my hands. "Get out of here. Both of you."

"Yes, ma'am." Nash playfully saluted me as he and Mo sauntered over toward her office.

For what was probably the millionth time, I reached into my desk drawer for my phone, hoping for a text from Rob, but there was nothing.

Damn.

As much as it pained me, it was probably time to move on. And going out tonight might help me get past the disappointment.

———

THE NEW CLUB we went to was nice. It was called Quest, and was a combination nightclub and restaurant. Dinner seating was limited, but the place was massive, decorated with a funky style of furnishings that gave it a steampunk vibe. I'd never been to a place like this before and it was as beautiful as it was interesting. Nirvana's "Come As You Are" was blasting from the loudspeakers in the main room, but our group was taken back to a reserved area in what could only be described as a mezzanine. It was up half a flight of stairs, with glass walls that allowed you to look down into the main part of the restaurant while simultaneously blocking out enough of the music to allow for conversation.

It was a medium-sized area, filled with a good mix of big and small tables. There were iron chandeliers and funky candleholders, combined with velvet furnishings and a variety of love seats and cushioned chairs. The decor was eclectic as hell, but everything was clean and new, giving it an expensive feel.

"This place is cool as shit," Nash said to me as we settled at one of the tables, along with Mo, Lars, his fiancée Sheridan, Boone, a woman Boone was dating named Fiona, and Konstantin.

"It really is," I agreed, looking around. "I'd been reading about the grand opening, so it's great we could get in here."

"Sheridan made a few calls," Nash said. "Thank god there's a supermodel in the family. Otherwise, there's a six-month waiting list for dinner reservations."

"Holy shit." My eyes widened. "That's nuts. I can't imagine there's any food I'd want to wait six months for."

"I don't think it's about the food," he mused, leaning back in his chair. "I think it's about being seen and mingling with the right people."

"Do you make it a point to mingle with the right people?" I asked quietly.

He shook his head. "Nah. I'm just a hockey player who happened to get offered a fuckton of money to do an underwear ad. Someday, I'm not gonna be able to play hockey anymore, so that's the kind of thing that helps me save for my future. Sure, I make great money now, but there are a lot of expenses too, and anyone who doesn't plan for something unexpected is taking a big risk."

Nash continued to surprise me. Every so often, the smart-ass hockey player took a back seat to a much more thoughtful, mature guy that I liked a lot more than I thought I would.

"That's smart," I said, nodding.

"Have you looked at this menu?" Sheridan called out. "It's as crazy as the decor."

"Oh, check it out," Nash said, opening his menu. "They have raclette."

"What is that?" I asked. It sounded vaguely familiar but I didn't think I'd ever tried it.

"It's awesome. It's both a type of cheese and the name of the appetizer that uses the cheese. Basically, you melt it and scrape it off the top. We have to get some. You'll love it."

"That sounds delicious."

"There's a great wine list too," Boone said. "Anyone interested in sharing a bottle of malbec?"

"I'm in," Nash nodded as he looked at me. "You?"

"Sure."

The waiter brought two bottles and glasses for our whole table. Conversation was light as we ate and drank. The raclette was one of the best things I'd ever put in my mouth and I couldn't help but ruminate over the different sides to Nash I kept discovering.

He was a loud, obnoxious professional athlete who was always planning pranks on his teammates, telling dirty jokes, and generally making a nuisance of himself. He was an amazing athlete, and from what I'd heard, a smart, hardworking teammate. He was also so good-looking it was hard to look away when he fixed those long-lashed blue eyes on you.

But then there was the other side of Nash. The

one who tirelessly signed postcards and other swag to help the team, charity, or almost anyone who asked, really. He was fiercely protective of his friends, enjoyed good food and wine, and I'd honestly never seen him moody or irritating. I'd seen his playful side, his serious side, and his professional side—and they were all on point. He was the whole damn package, which was confusing as hell because I usually avoided guys like him. Rich, successful, over-the-top-good-looking men were always trouble.

Always.

Right?

"Take the last bite," Nash said, scraping the last of the raclette off the plate and onto a piece of baguette.

My mouth opened before I could stop it and he popped the whole thing inside. I caught myself before closing my lips around his fingers, but it was almost too late. Our eyes met and the strike of lightning that flashed between us was impossible to miss.

I swallowed, reaching for my wine glass and downing what was left. I was absolutely not supposed to be flirting with Nash.

"You should tell me what you were thinking just now," he said under his breath.

"I don't think so." My face felt hot as he looked at

me. I wasn't sure if it was him or the wine making me feel this way, but damn, I would have given anything in that moment for him to touch me. The way he watched me told me he was thinking something similar, but neither of us seemed willing to make the first move.

Thank god.

The waiter refilled my glass and I took another sip, trying to still the wild beating of my heart. Why was he affecting me this way? I didn't like feeling so out of control, but months of hurt and rejection and stress had caught up to me. It was nice to be around someone so sexy who was also attentive. Someone who made me feel wanted. I wasn't insecure about myself, or my looks in general, but Theo had put a few nicks in the armor of my pride, and Mo had been right that it might be time to let my hair down.

The eight of us at our table finished off three bottles of wine before our main courses arrived, and I was pretty tipsy. We'd all taken Ubers from the arena, so I wasn't worried about driving, though I'd have to figure out how to get home if I didn't sober up soon in the next couple of hours.

"How's the steak?" Nash asked when our meals arrived.

"It's fantastic. Want a bite?" I'd just cut a piece and I offered it to him on my fork.

He opened his mouth and closed his lips around the tines of the fork, eyes never leaving mine as he slowly pulled away.

It might have been the most erotic thing I'd ever seen.

How was eating steak sexy? I wondered.

But with Nash it was.

Shit.

"That's delicious," he said, his voice a little lower and raspier than usual.

"Right?" I tried to counter by making mine light and nonchalant, but it was impossible. The chemistry between us tonight was practically tangible and the more we drank, the easier it became to allow myself to enjoy it.

"You have beautiful eyes," Nash said quietly, his mouth a fraction of an inch away from my ear.

"Th-thank you." I swallowed, turning to look at him.

He stared at me for a beat too long before asking, "Would you like to dance after we eat?"

"Yes."

Oh, fuck yes.

CHAPTER EIGHTEEN

Nash

"Where do we go from here?" I asked Sariah, my arousal making it hard to think straight.

The crowd at the club had thinned and we were two of the only people left. We'd had a couple more drinks as the night went on, but mostly we'd danced. When the music was on, we were on the floor together, our bodies finding an unspoken rhythm.

The DJ was done for the night now, and Sariah was standing across from me at a small high-top table, her cheeks flushed and her chest damp with sweat from dancing. She opened her mouth, closed it, and then opened it again.

"I don't know," she said, a note of apology in her

tone. "I mean, tonight has been great, but there's someone I really like and even though I think he just ghosted me…I'm in a weird place. And we work together. I like you, but I love my job, and I also need it."

I smiled as she continued talking herself in and out of taking things further with us. Her indecision was sexy as hell. Sariah was a smart woman who didn't act on impulse. She didn't have stars in her eyes over me, but I knew she wanted me every bit as much as I wanted her. I'd seen her nipples pebbled under her top as we danced, and I'd felt her soft exhales every time I put my hand on her hip.

"It's not that I wouldn't enjoy it," she reasoned, still debating with herself. "We both would, but—"

"Sariah," I said, stopping her. "Your place or mine?"

Her gaze locked with mine, her eyes glazed with desire. "Mine."

I took out my wallet and threw down enough cash to cover our drinks plus a tip, then took her hand and practically ran for the door, weaving around the chairs that had been left pulled out from tables.

"Heels!" Sariah said through laughter from behind me. "I can't run in heels!"

That was an easy problem to solve. I turned, slid

an arm behind her neck and another under her knees and picked her up. She yelped and wrapped her arms around my neck, holding on for dear life.

"I won't be of much use to you later if you choke me to death," I quipped.

"Where are we even going?"

"Your place, remember?"

"We don't have a car," she reminded me.

"I'll call an Uber when we get outside."

Everyone else we'd come here with had left the club hours ago. Mo had winked at me on her way out, clearly wise to how I'd been hoping tonight would end.

I set Sariah's feet on the ground and took out my phone to order an Uber. She grabbed her phone from her bag and checked the screen, sighing softly before putting it away.

Was she hoping for a text from Rob? Probably. It had burned when she said there was someone she really liked who had left her high and dry. I hadn't meant to hurt her, but when she'd said she wanted to meet Rob, I froze. Obviously that couldn't happen if I wanted to have a chance with her, and I really fucking wanted that. I was hoping she'd fall for me and down the road, over an intimate dinner, I'd tell her the truth. Not before she'd been thoroughly charmed, though.

"Everything okay?" I asked her.

"Yeah, just…" She took a deep breath and exhaled, smiling up at me. "Yeah. Everything's okay."

It was trippy that I was competing *with myself* for Sariah's affection, but I couldn't get hung up on that in this moment. I wanted to focus all my attention on her.

"I loved dancing with you tonight," I said, taking her hand.

"Me too."

A breeze blew past us and ruffled a few strands of her dark hair, blowing them across her face. I'd been admiring her beauty all night, completely mesmerized by her. She moved a hand up to brush the strands away, but I beat her to it, cupping her cheek once I'd tucked the hair behind her ear.

In that moment, I couldn't wait another second. I lowered my lips to hers and rested my free hand on her hip. As I kissed her, she pressed her body against mine, getting closer as our kiss deepened. I felt myself growing hard behind the fly of my pants, my erection pressing against her stomach.

She tasted sweet, like the wine she'd been drinking tonight. Her mouth was warm, and the more I took from it the more I wanted. As she moved her hands up my neck to grip at the ends of my hair, I heard a voice calling out my name. I ignored it, only to hear it again.

"Nash?" a male voice yelled.

Sariah and I turned, both of us breathless and slightly dazed.

"Yeah?" I said, irritated by the interruption.

"I'm your Uber driver," he said, shaking his head. "No sex acts allowed in the car."

Sariah burst out laughing, and I did, too.

"Damn him," I cracked. "He just ruined my plan to seduce you in the back of his Chevy."

We got into the car and tried to make small talk with the driver, but he'd been over us since catching us making out on the sidewalk. He kept checking his rearview mirror to make sure we weren't fucking our brains out in his back seat.

It was a good thing I hadn't driven here tonight. Not just because I'd had quite a bit to drink, but also because I couldn't remember ever being this worked up over a woman. I couldn't focus on anything but Sariah. She'd let her guard down tonight, and this side of her was irresistible.

On the fifteen-minute ride to her apartment, I said many silent prayers that she wouldn't change her mind about me. If only she knew I was every-thing she liked about Rob *and* everything she liked about Nash.

Based on the deuces he threw up as he drove away, I could tell the driver was glad to be rid of us. I felt the same way, because now it was just Sariah and me as we made our way toward her apartment building.

Though it was dark, I could tell her building was nice. It had a modern, clean design and immaculate landscaping. Even now, a set of sprinklers watered the grass, a few droplets hitting us as we walked to her door.

"It's a mess," she said as she unlocked it. "You know, moving mode and all."

"I don't care about any of that," I said, taking her by the hips and pulling her to me. "This right here is all I care about."

I kissed her again, sliding my hands down to cup her ass and groaning with need from the feel of it. She waved an arm out, trying to close the front door, but not able to reach it.

In one quick movement, I pushed the door closed and picked her up, eliciting a gasp from her as her legs instinctively wrapped around my waist.

"Bedroom," I said, no hesitation in my command. We were going there, and we were going *now*.

"Second door on the right," she murmured.

I held her tightly as I made my way to the hallway, stopping to press her against the wall and kiss the absolute fuck out of her. She tightened the hold of her legs around me, her hips grinding into mine as our mouths devoured each other.

Bedroom. This was our first time, and I wasn't going to let myself come from dry fucking her against a wall. Reluctantly, I started walking again.

"Promise this won't change anything with us at work," she said, her hands in my hair and her teeth grazing my earlobe.

"It won't."

"But—"

I squeezed her ass, turning her protest into a moan. When I set her on the bed, I put a knee on the mattress, leaning down to kiss her softly.

"Don't think so much," I said against her lips. "For a few hours, just *feel*." I put my hand over her heart. "This is what really matters."

Her eyes widened and she nodded. I stripped my shirt off and lowered my mouth to her neck, kissing and nipping in exploration, searching out all of her sweet spots. Every moan of satisfaction sent a bolt of arousal to my painfully swollen cock.

All I wanted was to touch and taste every inch of her. I slowly peeled away her top, pants, and bra, almost losing it when I flicked my tongue across a hard nipple and watched her shiver in delight.

She was doing the same to me—running her

hands over every inch of skin as she uncovered it. When I was down to just my boxers, she slipped her hand inside and wrapped it around my cock, making me groan hard.

Goddamn. It had been a while since I'd last had sex, but I'd gone without before and not felt like a teenager being touched for the first time. Sariah did something to me that no woman ever had before.

"I don't have condoms," she whispered.

"I do."

"Thank god. Get one. I need you to get one now."

My heart raced with desire as she spoke. As I looked around for a condom in my wallet, I said, "What do you mean you *need* me to?"

"You know what I mean."

I slid off my boxers and ripped open the condom package. "But I still want to hear you say it."

After a beat of silence, she said, "I need…you." So quiet it was almost indiscernible, she added, "Inside me."

"Baby, the sound of you saying that is almost too much." I rolled on the condom and then slid her panties down, pressing a kiss to the neatly trimmed strip of curls between her legs. "I need it, too. I need to show you what you do to me. I need to make you come. Say my name when you do, and I won't last another second."

As I pushed the tip of my cock inside her, she inhaled sharply. I sank in slowly, her tight pussy testing my control with every inch. Her long, low moan of satisfaction forced me to grab a handful of the pillow her head was resting on and squeeze it with every ounce of strength I could muster.

We quickly found a rhythm, moving slowly together at first, but when I began to move faster, Sariah's hips matched mine, her breathing getting shallower and shallower.

"God…I'm close," she breathed. "Don't stop."

I pumped my hips harder and faster, feeling her getting closer, and her legs tightened around my waist as she cried out.

"Nash, oh god!"

"Come hard for me, baby," I urged. "Grind that pussy on my cock."

Her hips shot up as she moaned loud and long, my cock begging for its own release. As soon as she started to come down, I drove myself into her a final time, groaning raggedly as I came. She cupped my face as I found my breath again, and I moved my lips over hers in a chaste kiss.

"That was…intense," she said.

"Yeah." I pulled out of her and lay on my back, wrapping my arm around her and pulling her close.

She curled against my side, laughing softly.

"I can't believe that just happened."

"Why not?" I ran my thumb in slow circles over her arm.

"I think it's just crazy that I just slept with the guy I answer fan mail for. The guy who gets panties and poems sent to him."

"None of that means anything to me. I mean, I appreciate it, but it doesn't change my opinion of myself."

"Because it's already as high as one's opinion can get," she cracked.

"Hey, I'm not a bad catch." I kissed her temple. "And you could write a poem for me if you wanted to."

"Hmm…let's see. Okay, how about this? I met a guy named Nash, and he had a lot of cash. Turns out he's not all flash, and we're gonna eat some hash…browns."

I laughed and kissed her lightly. "Are you saying you're hungry?"

"Starving."

"I'll make us some food. And then we're coming right back to this bed for round two."

"Agreed, but where's my poem?"

I considered her question, knowing that I'd never in my life written a poem. So I decided to wing it, like she had.

"I met a girl named Sariah, and she's not a liah."

She laughed, and I continued, feeling encouraged.

"Damn is she fine, and can she ever sixty-nine." I quickly winked at her before grabbing her hand and leading her down the hallway to the kitchen.

"Nice. I guess I know what you have planned for round two."

Hell. Yeah.

CHAPTER NINETEEN

Sariah

IT HAD BEEN a long time since I woke up to a warm, hard body pressed against me in bed. Theo had liked to sprawl out, meaning he was usually diagonal in the bed by morning, sheets and blankets everywhere, his body as far away from mine as possible. Nash was the opposite, having stayed practically glued to me all night long. Even when we weren't having sex. And there had been a lot of sex.

When we ran out of condoms, we showered and switched to oral, and that was pretty much the end of me. I'd never come so hard, or so many times, and still wanted more. He was the most generous and giving lover I'd ever been with, but in the light of day, I suddenly didn't know what to do. While my body still basked in what I could only describe as a sensual, tingling afterglow, my brain was in overload.

Now he knew where I lived.

Now I'd have to look at him at work almost every day.

Now he might think I was interested in more than sex.

Ugh.

What had I been thinking?

I slid out from under his arm and hurried to the bathroom. I had to be at work in less than an hour and my hair was a wild halo around my head. A quick shower and a few minutes with the blow-dryer would tame my hair. Then I'd figure out how to get out of the apartment with the least amount of awkwardness once I was done getting ready.

The water sluiced over me and I closed my eyes. I only had a few minutes to luxuriate in hot water and condition my hair, so I tried not to think about the Adonis asleep in my bed. I'd glanced over my shoulder on my way to the bathroom and mentally confirmed he was the sexiest man alive. And lying there naked in my bed didn't hurt either.

I started as strong arms wrapped around my waist from behind.

"Didn't mean to scare you." His voice was thick from sleep, but his touch was light as his fingers skimmed my belly.

"Good morning," I murmured, leaning into him even as my brain screamed no. My body had a mind of its own, though, and when he kissed the soft spot behind my ear, I sighed.

"Were you planning to sneak out of your own apartment?" he asked in a playful tone, the fingers of one hand traveling down to the apex of my thighs.

"N-no…" I sighed and let my eyes close again. "Just have to get ready for work—Nash!" I squealed as he slid a finger inside of me.

"You know we don't need condoms for me to make you feel good."

"Mmm." I groaned as he nudged my thighs apart and began circling my clit with his fingers.

"You're already wet."

"I can't imagine why," I murmured.

He used his hand to cup my mound, squeezing a little and then sliding two fingers inside of me. The heel of his palm was pressed against my clit as he finger fucked me and within a couple of minutes, I was surging against his hand. I came with a soft cry, shuddering against his strong chest.

"If I could start every day watching you come like

that, my life would be pretty fucking perfect," he said, kissing the side of my neck.

Oh, geez.

What was I doing? I'd been trying to sneak away from him, not let him seduce me all over again.

"I have to go to work," I whispered, though I was still pressed tightly against him, my back to his front.

"I know. Me too. Just a couple more minutes." He rested his chin on my shoulder. "I had a great time last night, Sariah."

"Me too."

Shit, this was it. The moment where he'd say he wanted to see me again or send me packing. Since I didn't want to deal with either of those scenarios, I forced myself to pull away and began rinsing the conditioner out of my hair. When I was finished, I leaned up on my toes and pressed a light kiss to his lips.

"I'm sorry to rush off, but I have to get going." I stepped out of the shower before he could stop me and wrapped myself in a towel.

Instead of waiting for him, I hurried into my closet to pick out clothes. My closet was pretty bare these days, with most of my clothes packed into suitcases so I could take them over to the new apartment as soon as I got the key.

I grabbed dark-gray slacks, a pale-pink button-down blouse, and a nude-colored bra and panty set. I'd just stepped into my panties when I heard movement behind me. I turned to find Nash lounging against the doorway of the closet, a towel wrapped low on his hips.

Jesus. Fucking. Christ.

His shoulders took up most of the doorway and the light trail of hair on his torso that disappeared into the towel reminded me of what it felt like to have him inside of me.

"You okay?" he asked quietly, his eyes searching my face.

"I'm fine." I put on my bra and started buttoning my blouse. "Just running a little late. Would you do me a favor? Go into the kitchen and turn on my Keurig? It's getting old and takes a while to warm up these days."

He hesitated for a second but then nodded, disappearing from view.

I got dressed as quickly as I could and then brushed out the tangles in my hair. Rustling in the bedroom told me Nash was getting dressed too. I'd just pulled out my blow-dryer when he came into the bathroom.

"Listen, I have to stop at home before I go to practice, but I'll see you at work, okay?"

"Yes. Sure." I nodded but then a thought occurred to me. "Nash?"

"Yeah?"

"You don't think anyone…saw us? Leaving the club, I mean."

"They definitely saw us dancing, but everyone was gone by the time we left."

"Can you, uh, keep this between us, please? I don't want to be the source of office gossip."

"I would never do that," he said, coming over to me. He rested a hand on the side of my face. "You can trust me, Sariah. I would never do anything to hurt you. Professionally or otherwise."

I gazed up into his handsome face and the sincerity in his eyes made me want to throw myself against his chest and hold on tightly. But I couldn't. Or at least I wouldn't. This was just the aftermath of incredible sex and I wasn't so young or naive to believe it could be anything more.

"Thank you. I'll see you later."

"We're going to talk about all of this," he said slowly. "But we both have to get going so it can't be right now."

"We don't have to talk about anything," I whispered. "It's all good."

Then I turned on the blow-dryer, effectively eliminating further conversation.

He watched me for a moment before leaning over to kiss my cheek and heading out.

———

I'D JUST GOTTEN to my desk when Mo came over and perched on her favorite corner.

"You. Me. Lunch. Today."

I chuckled. "Okay."

"I want every detail, girlfriend."

"I don't know what you're talking about," I said, powering on my computer and avoiding her eyes. I already knew I'd tell her about last night, but not now. And definitely not here.

"Girl, don't make me drag it out of you."

I managed not to smile. "What time do you want to go to lunch?"

"Eleven thirty?"

I laughed. "Sure. Where are we going?"

"I was thinking about the new…" Her voice trailed off as she stared at something in the hallway.

I twisted in my chair to see what it was and frowned. There was a guy I'd never seen before laughing with Lance and Kevin. He was probably in his late twenties, with dark hair and a gorgeous smile. He was good-looking but Mo seemed mesmerized.

"Who is that?" I asked her.

"Knox Bachmann. He's a scout for the team, and he is *fine*. Makes my heart go pitter-patter just looking at him."

"You definitely need to get laid."

"You can say that again." She got up and started to walk back to her office, but paused and turned back. "Just tell me one thing. How was it on a scale of one to ten?"

I didn't even look up from my computer. "Eleven point three."

She was still hooting with laughter when she closed the door to her office.

I tried to focus on work, but my mind kept straying to last night.

Nash and I on the dance floor, moving together so naturally it was like we'd danced before.

Nash kissing me, his big hands playing my body like a musical instrument.

Nash inside of me.

I mentally groaned, dropping my head and closing my eyes.

I shouldn't be thinking about him.

This morning had been less awkward than I'd thought it would be but more awkward than I would have liked. He said we needed to talk, which could mean just about anything, and I hated being in this position. I'd let wine and raging hormones overtake my better judgment last night and now I was going to have to be around him at the office. God forbid he told anyone.

There was no formal rule with the Mavericks about employees dating, but it still wasn't professional. I was a woman in the very male-dominated field of professional sports, so sleeping with one of the players wasn't a good look.

I had to make sure Nash understood that we couldn't do that ever again. I had a job and a reputation to think of, and he probably wasn't interested in anything serious anyway. Once I pointed out that the only way we could date was if we were serious, he'd definitely back off. A professional athlete like Nash undoubtedly had girlfriends in every city the team played in, and he wouldn't give all that up for me. No matter how good the sex was.

Feeling better about my decision, I focused on work until Mo and I went to lunch. We had a good time and it reminded me that I hadn't spoken to Dee in over a week. I saw even less of her now that I worked for the Mavericks and a tiny bit of guilt crept in. I'd been so busy talking to Rob, spending time with my new friends within the Mavericks organization, and lusting after Nash, I hadn't made time for my best friend. Which was a shitty thing to do, especially since she'd requested a day off work to help me move in just over a week.

"Invite her next time we go out," Mo said when I mentioned it to her. "And if she's your bestie, she'll understand. You've had a lot going on."

"Oh, I know. I just was never the type of woman who would put a man over her girlfriends."

"Technically, you're not. We've gone out, what, three or four times since you started here? All you do is work, occasionally see your family, and pack. You deserved a night like last night and she'll understand. Then you'll bring her along when we go out, she'll be surrounded by hot hockey players, and she'll forget all about it."

We laughed as we got off the elevator.

"Okay, I have work to do," I told her. "See you later."

"Bye." She went toward her office and I sat down at my desk.

"Hey, did you hear the news?" Kevin looked up from his laptop.

I shook my head. "What news?"

"Sawyer Cain's wife died."

Nash

I SWITCHED OFF MY RADIO, deciding to finish my drive to the arena in silence. The lyrics to every song were getting to me this morning.

Just after arriving at my house to shower and let my dogs out, I'd gotten a call from Wes telling me that Annie Cain had died late last night. Or early this morning I guess. The whole thing felt so surreal.

It was also just fucking unfair. She was a sweet woman who had been ravaged by cancer and fought hard to reach remission, and she had, for a while. But the cancer came back with a vengeance, and it took her quickly.

Sawyer had to have known, but he didn't let on

how bad the situation with Annie's health had been. It was crushing to imagine what that was like for him. Wes said on the phone that Sawyer had told him she wasn't doing well, but she'd passed away faster than the doctors had predicted.

Every time my mind wandered to thoughts about Sariah's warm body in my arms last night, or the way her little laughs and sighs of pleasure lit me up from the inside out, my mind went to my teammate Sawyer. He'd never hear his wife's laugh again, or hear her voice wish him good luck. When he was on the road, they talked on the phone constantly. There was no filling the void that had just swallowed up a huge part of his world.

"Mornin', Mr. Reilly," the parking attendant at the arena said to me, touching the brim of his hat.

"Morning, Moses."

"Pretty sad one today."

Moses had been working for the Warren Center for many years; he was part of the family here. Usually he had a huge grin on his face, but not today.

"She was a bright light, wasn't she?" I asked.

The corners of his lips tipped up in a smile. "That she was, sir. I'm gonna miss that beautiful smile."

"Me too."

"You guys win that game tonight for her, you hear?"

"Yes, sir. I know she and Sawyer will be on everyone's mind."

After parking in the player lot, I steeled myself before walking through the player entrance. I kept my head down on the walk to the locker room, not in the mood for the usual grins and fist bumps.

The last time I saw Annie was when several teammates met up for dinner at Giovanna's Italian Bistro. Her hair had grown back, and even though it was short, it was obvious that having her own hair back meant a lot to her. I'd noticed her running her hands over it and smiling several times while she, and Lars's girlfriend Sheridan, had thrown back a couple bottles of wine together, laughing like only close girlfriends did.

When I walked into the locker room, it was quiet. The usual level of excitement expected on the day of a playoff game was nowhere to be found.

"Hey," Wes said.

"Hey."

"Obviously, Sawyer's out for tonight."

I lowered my brows. "He's out for the rest of the playoffs, isn't he? His wife just died."

Wes shrugged. "That's not my call. Depends how far we make it, I guess."

"Have you talked to him? How is he?"

"He's…" Wes shook his head. "She died in their

bed, man. He woke up in the middle of the night and she was just gone. The doctors aren't sure what happened."

"Holy shit. So he didn't even…?"

"Yeah, it wasn't like when you know it's coming. I mean, they knew, but they thought she still had a little time left. So he's not just devastated, but shocked, too. He's got family at the house with him, but he's a mess."

"We should go by this afternoon and see him."

Wes scrunched his face, not fully agreeing with my idea. "I don't know."

"Why?"

"For one, I don't want to draw any attention to him. If reporters followed us—"

I scrubbed a hand down my face. "It's fucking insane that those vultures would want to snap pictures at a time like this."

"I know. But you know how they are."

"Yeah, I just…I don't know. I want him to know we're here for him."

Wes nodded. "I do, too. I talked to Coach about it earlier and he said we'll make the time if some of us want to visit today."

"What do you think?"

Wes ran a hand through his hair, looking pained. "I don't fucking know, man. Ben would know exactly what to do, but I just keep going back and forth."

I put a hand on his shoulder. "Ben would feel the same way you do. You know how Ben approached things—he ran through the pros and cons and then made a call. And he was the first one to admit that sometimes there's no perfect answer."

He looked from side to side, making sure there was no one listening. "Sheridan is over at Sawyer's, and she told Lars he's a wreck. I don't know if we're supposed to show up and support him, or give him some privacy."

"What if we don't all go?" I suggested. "It could just be you, or you and a couple of other guys."

Wes nodded. "That might be better."

"He'll have family there to run interference if he's not up to seeing us. But we at least need to show up and let him know we care."

"Will you come with me?" he asked. "And I'll ask Lars, too."

"Of course."

This was Sawyer's first season on the team, and he had been standoffish at first, but once the team found out about Annie's health, they both had been pulled into the team fold immediately. I didn't know what we would say to him, but showing up and not knowing what to say was better than not showing up at all.

———

"IT WAS nice of you to come," a woman with red-rimmed eyes said as she opened the door to Sawyer and Annie's house.

Their home was an older, immaculately maintained two-story made of stone, with bright flowers spilling out of large planters on either side of the wooden front door.

"We're very sorry for your loss," Wes said as we stepped inside.

"Thank you. I'm Sawyer's mom, Lisa."

We all introduced ourselves and shook hands with Lisa. Wes stepped back out to the front porch and brought in a large box he'd set down.

"This is from the team. It's some meals you guys can freeze if you need to and a bunch of gift cards if you want to get takeout. Should be plenty to get you through the next couple of weeks."

Lisa's eyes filled with tears. "How thoughtful of you guys. Thank you."

"Want me to carry it into the kitchen?" Wes asked.

"Yes, that would be a big help."

Sheridan walked into the living room, looking casual in sweatpants and a T-shirt, her dark hair up in a ponytail. Her eyes were swollen and her face was red, and as soon as she saw Lars, she burst into tears and ran toward him.

"I'm here now, love," Lars said, embracing her and resting his cheek on top of her head.

Dude had grown by leaps and bounds since meeting Sheridan. He had recently been diagnosed with autism, and while the news had hit him hard, he'd since become confident in who he was. He'd recently told me his enhanced ability to compartmentalize because of his autism was an asset when he was reviewing film before games. When Lars had a mind to, he could hone in on one thing with more focus than anyone I knew.

"Hey, Nash," Sheridan said, wiping her face and coming over to hug me.

"Hey, Sheridan. I'm really sorry for your loss."

"It fucking sucks. It's true what they say about only the good dying young. Annie was—" Her expression crumbled and she broke down in tears again.

Lars wrapped her back up in his arms. I met his gaze, wishing I knew what to say.

Several people came down from upstairs and introduced themselves. I met Annie's brother and sister-in-law, Annie's parents, and one of Sawyer's best friends.

Wes came back into the living room and we were all standing around talking when Sawyer walked downstairs. As soon as he saw the three of us, his eyes welled with tears. My throat tightened as Wes embraced Sawyer. It was devastating seeing my tall, broad-shouldered, seemingly fearless teammate crying so hard that his shoulders shook.

"We all loved her," Wes said.

He was crying, too. Hell, we all were. I wiped at the corners of my eyes and hugged Sawyer.

"I'm so sorry, man. I wish I knew something better to say."

"Nothing helps, anyway," Sawyer said, pulling away from me and embracing Lars.

"What can we do for you?" Wes asked him. "Anything you need."

Sawyer shook his head. "I don't know. I appreciate you guys coming. I don't know when I'll be back. I know it's the playoffs, but—"

"Hockey's just a game," I said, interrupting him. "Annie was your whole life. Take the time you need."

He nodded, looking numb. "I can't imagine ever playing again. I can't imagine…"

When he broke down again, his mom came over and put an arm around him.

"This isn't the time for anything but grieving," she said softly. "You don't need to do anything else."

Sawyer nodded, wiping his hands across his cheeks and composing himself. Then he held his hand out to Wes for a handshake.

"I want to thank you for the way you welcomed us when we came here," he said solemnly. "Hadley and Sheridan were the first friends Annie had here, and the past six months—" Tears welled in his eyes and he cleared his throat. "We felt like we had family here. Going to games and cookouts and birthday parties…it meant a lot to Annie. Thank you for that."

"You guys *do* have family here," Wes said. "I meant it when I said we're here for whatever you need. We'll be checking up on you so much it gets annoying."

Sawyer smiled. "I'm used to you guys annoying me."

My gaze landed on a wall of framed photos. Sawyer and Annie on their wedding day, looking into each other's faces adoringly. The two of them with a dog. Annie standing in a field of sunflowers, smiling radiantly, with a bright pink scarf covering her head.

Fuck. It was like a punch in the gut for *me* to look at those pictures, so I could only imagine what that would feel like for Sawyer in the days and weeks to come.

"I'll be watching the game tonight," Sawyer said. "Win it, okay? I appreciate you guys coming by. Sorry I'm such a mess."

"Don't apologize," Wes said. "You'll be with us in spirit, and Annie will be, too."

Sawyer nodded, looking unsure and lost.

Lars clapped him on the shoulder and said something in Swedish. It was rare for him to speak in his native tongue, and we all listened in earnest.

"That is a proverb that means shared joys are doubled and shared sorrows are halved," he said to Sawyer. "We are here to share in your sorrow, my friend, now and always."

Sometimes Lars butchered the English language; other times, he was more eloquent than I could ever be.

"Love you, man," I said to Sawyer, embracing him again.

We left then, taking note of and ignoring the photographers trying to snap photos from the end of Sawyer's privacy gate. We drove back to the arena in near silence, and as we pulled in, there were more photographers waiting.

"Game faces, boys," Wes said. "Let's do this."

CHAPTER TWENTY-ONE

Sariah

I HADN'T KNOWN Annie Cain, but my heart broke for everyone in the Mavericks organization that did. Monique had been quiet and teary-eyed for most of the morning, and even the sales guys seemed subdued. Monique was putting together a short video tribute that would be shown tonight at the game in Annie's honor, and it was hard to believe the beautiful, vibrant young woman in all the pictures was dead. And poor Sawyer. I couldn't fathom what he was going through right now.

Nash had come up with my midmorning Starbucks, but even though he smiled and we chatted for a few minutes, he definitely wasn't himself. Those who had offices stayed in them, mostly behind closed doors, and the rest of us did our best to hold down the fort. I spent most of the day answering the phone since so many of my colleagues sounded too depressed to take sales calls. It was good in a way, because it kept me busy and distracted. I might not have known Annie, but Sawyer came around now and then, just like the others, signing postcards and doing whatever he could to help us sell ticket packages.

Tonight was the first playoff game, though, so everyone had to buck up. Jackson Athletics was sponsoring a hot dog eating contest between the first and second period, and I'd thought everything was handled for that. Until I saw the promo photo. After nearly pissing my pants, I made a beeline for the art department at the ripe hour of four p.m.

"Teri, is this a joke?" I asked, walking into the office of the director of art and media.

"Um…what?" she asked, not even looking up from her computer.

"Teri." I put the mock-up I'd printed out down in front of her. "Is it a hot dog eating contest or soft porn night at the Mavericks game?"

She blinked, as if seeing the photo for the first time. It showed a young teenage girl staring at a hot dog, eyes wide and lips parted like she was on the verge of going down on it.

"I don't…" Her voice trailed off. "Jesus fucking Christ. I never saw this. I was out the last two days—my kids are sick—so I told Manny to handle it. Fuck fuck fuck."

"Can we just reshoot it?"

"The game starts in three hours! Where are we going to find a model? Shit, I could get fired for this. I have two kids in braces; I can't get fired."

"We'll figure it out. Don't you know anyone? What about one of the guys on the team?" I immediately thought of Nash, but he was a wreck right now, and he had enough pressure to play tonight. I couldn't imagine asking him to do something like this.

"After what happened to Sawyer's wife, I don't think so." She was rummaging through an old-school Rolodex.

"How long have you had that?" I asked curiously, since the only other person I knew who still had one was my old managing editor at the newspaper, who was in his sixties.

Teri smiled. "My husband gave it to me the day I got my first job out of college. It's more sentimental than practical."

I smiled back. "Well, hopefully, you'll pull a rabbit out of that dinosaur."

"I got nothin'," Teri muttered. "I don't really deal in models because we use very few. Most of our program covers are either players or the mascot, and the vendors usually provide their own."

"Well, we better think of something because the doors open in just under two hours and a Twitter mob could make an entire comedy routine out of this photo."

She squinted up at me, carefully looking me up and down.

"What?" I asked in alarm, looking down to see if there was a stain on my shirt or something.

"You were Miss Teen Missouri and you've got cheekbones to die for. This is right up your alley!"

"Me?" I squeaked. "No. My modeling days are long gone. No way."

"We're desperate and you qualify. Go touch up your makeup."

"No, I don't think—" I was cut off as Teri got up and nudged me toward the door.

"Desperate times, desperate measures and all that. Think of my two kids in braces and my youngest, whose teeth are going in seventeen different directions already. Go. I'll round up one of the photographers and we'll knock out a new promo still in ten minutes."

Good grief.

I spent so much time avoiding the limelight and now I was being thrust back into it whether I wanted to or not. For hot dog porn, no less. Despite the situation, I chuckled. I was going to ask for a bonus for doing this.

I grabbed my purse, hoping I had enough makeup to make myself presentable and I'd just gotten to the ladies' room when I felt my phone buzz in my pocket. To my shock, there was a text from Rob.

ROB: Hey. I'm sorry it took me so long to respond. I didn't mean to be a douche, but I just can't meet you in person and I can't tell you why. Believe me, it has nothing to do with you. There's just some shit I have to handle first. Take care, Rob.

I stared at it for a little too long, a plethora of emotions washing over me. Sadness that he didn't want to meet in person, frustration that he wouldn't tell me why, and anger that I'd invested so much of myself in this strange relationship. Was he married? Otherwise involved with someone and now having regrets?

Ugh. Men sucked.

I couldn't change him or his feelings, though, so I'd pull up my big-girl panties and move on.

———

THERE WASN'T a dry eye in the house when they did the video tribute to Annie just before the game started. Even some of the stodgy veteran sports reporters in the press corps seemed misty-eyed, and that was saying something. The crowd was respectful, but in all honesty, the tribute was more for those of us in the Mavericks organization than anything else, so seconds after it was over, the volume in the arena hit eleven. People were on their feet and from where I sat in the concourse, the hot dog eating contest was going to be a hoot.

The money would go to charity and everyone who participated got swag and discount coupons for Jackson Athletics. With my face all over the jumbotron and at the booth where people were signing up, I was in the spotlight much more than I wanted to be, but at least the picture of me holding a hot dog in each hand was tame and G-rated compared to the original photo. They'd photo-shopped in a hot dog cart, giving it a carnival feel, so it made it a lot more innocent.

I got in the elevator and headed up. I liked

watching from the press box since it was big and airy, set at center ice. The arena was sold out tonight, and though that wasn't unusual, it felt good to know I helped make it happen.

This job fulfilled me in ways none of my others ever had. Not only was the money good, but I looked forward to coming in every day. I'd made friends, my colleagues respected me, and the bonuses would make my life so much easier.

The puck dropped and my heart was instantly in my throat. I was always happy and a little nervous when the Mavericks played, but this was different. I was excited in general, but I was also a little enamored watching Nash on the ice. I knew the cocky prankster side of him, the thoughtful, generous side, and now the sexy, passionate side. There was so much more to him than I'd imagined and seeing what he was capable of on the ice made me reconsider everything I thought I knew about him.

How was one professional athlete the whole fucking package and how had I allowed myself to fall under his spell? I didn't have any illusions about us having a future or anything crazy like that, but my gut told me neither of us had gotten enough of the sex.

A breakaway on the ice snapped my attention back to the game and Nash glided toward Tampa's net like he and the puck were one. He flicked his wrist and the puck slid between the goalie's legs, and when that red light went off I screamed as loud as everyone else.

"Way to score, Reilly!" I yelled out.

"Bet you liked when he scored last night too," Monique murmured in my ear.

My face flushed hot and I jabbed her with my elbow. "Hush!" I replied in a heated whisper. We'd been too busy to go to lunch, but we'd snuck away for a quick break where I'd given her the *Reader's Digest* version of last night's sexcapades.

She just laughed at me. "Go on down and play with those wieners."

I gave her a look. "Are you sure you're not a thirteen-year-old boy?"

"Sometimes."

Despite her ribbing, the game was action packed and the hot dog eating contest went well. We had over fifty contestants and the winner got four tickets to the game of their choice next season.

I missed the second goal, scored by Wes, but Nash scored again just as I got back up to the press box and the energy in the arena was contagious.

"That's how you do it, Reilly!" Monique said, putting two fingers in her mouth and whistling louder than anyone I'd ever heard in my life.

"Damn, you got some lungs," I said, laughing.

Despite today's tragic loss, the team was on fire. They were focused and steady, keeping Tampa on their toes, and Drew was like a brick wall in goal. He made saves that left us gasping, and as the final buzzer sounded, the team immediately surrounded him. There was no doubt he was tonight's first star, and I watched the celebrations on the ice and in the stands with a smile.

Hopefully, we would go out to celebrate.

My body still tingled from last night's lovemaking, and I would have been a liar if I said I didn't want more. I was an adult who was allowed to enjoy mind-blowing sex with the sexiest man alive, and after all the sadness today, I was pretty sure Nash could use some too. I'd think about what it might mean for us to continue sleeping together later. Right now, I just wanted to party.

I headed down to the lower level looking for Monique. The team was probably showering and getting dressed now, so it would be a little while before I could see Nash, but Mo would know if people were going out.

"Hey, give me five, will you?" she called out. She was huddled with two of the camera operators and I nodded.

"Come find me," I called back. I headed toward

the family lounge, which was on the same level as the locker rooms, smiling at friends and family members I recognized. I felt a little out of place, since I technically wasn't a friend or family member, so I leaned against a wall and pulled out my phone, checking email.

"Hey, Sariah."

I looked up, surprised to see Eric Alvarado standing there. I barely knew him and we'd never exchanged more than a few hellos.

"Hi, Eric."

"I wanted to talk to you about something. You have a minute?"

"Sure. What's up?"

"Not here." He headed around the corner to where the coaching staff offices were, and a bit quieter. The hallway was empty since everyone was busy with the press and such, and I wondered what this was about.

"What's going on?" I asked him.

"This is kind of awkward," he said, scratching his chin. "But I feel bad, so I figured I should tell you."

"Tell me what?"

"I overheard something in the locker room, and I normally wouldn't rat out my teammates, but what Nash is doing is inappropriate."

My stomach clenched painfully as I could only

imagine what Nash had told his teammates about last night. I never dreamed he would do something so vile.

I was going to kill him.

"So…" He cleared his throat.

"What about Nash?" I felt like I might puke but I wouldn't let him see how terrified I was.

"You've been talking to some guy online named Rob, right?"

How the fuck did Eric know about Rob?!

I could only stare, completely blindsided. "H-how do you know that?"

"Because Rob is really Nash."

Our eyes met and I squinted. "What?"

He blew out a breath. "I heard him telling one of the other guys how he had this scam going with you. At first I thought it was kind of harmless and fun, none of my business, but then I heard you guys were getting cozy at the club and I realized it wasn't just an online thing anymore."

"I…" There were no words because my chest felt like it was on fire. "I don't believe you," I said at last.

He shrugged. "Ask him. You can also check the phone number you have for Rob against the team directory. You'll see I'm telling the truth. Anyway, I thought you should know. Do what you want with the information." He turned and headed back toward the lounge, and I stared after him, sick and horrified and furious.

I took a moment to gather my thoughts and then I followed in the direction Eric had gone.

Nash and Lars were coming down the hall laughing, and I walked right up to him, my heart hammering against my rib cage.

"You and I have to talk," I hissed. "Right. Fucking. Now."

Lars gave Nash a funny look but quickly walked away and Nash frowned.

"What's wrong?" he asked. "Are you okay?"

I stared at him. "Do you have dogs, Nash?"

He looked confused. "Uh, what?"

"Simple question. Do. You. Have. Dogs."

He swallowed, his Adam's apple bobbing up and down. "Uh, yeah."

"How many?"

"Sariah, what—"

"Just answer the fucking question."

He looked sheepish as he answered, which was an answer in itself. "Three."

"Archie, Louie, and Athena, right?" If we'd been anywhere else, I would have slapped him across the face. "You son of a bitch."

"Sariah—"

"I can't believe it. Eric was telling the truth."

Nash's gaze narrowed and he scowled. "What the fuck did Eric tell you?"

"That you're Rob. *My* Rob. The Rob I've been texting for two months. And you're a lying bastard." My fists were clenched at my side.

"I was going to tell you," he whispered, reaching for my arm.

I wrenched it away from him before he could touch me. "Don't fucking touch me."

"Sariah, please let me explain…" He looked sad and genuinely contrite, but that wasn't my problem. Not after what he'd done.

I turned on my heel and headed for the elevators.

I was a thousand percent done with Nash fucking Reilly.

CHAPTER TWENTY-TWO

Nash

"Come on, Sariah, we need to talk. I was an asshole
and I fully admit that. I'm sorry and I just want to
explain. Call me back."

I ended the call, put the phone back in my pocket
and walked back into the bar the team was celebrating at. Since Sariah confronted me after the
game, I'd sent around a dozen texts and left two
voice mails, but she was ignoring me.

Fuck. I should've told her. In all the times I'd
imagined clever ways to tell her once she was thoroughly taken by me in a couple of months, I'd never
considered she'd find out like this.

Eric Alvarado was going to be sorry. What I'd been doing to him so far was just hazing a rookie for funsies, but he'd crossed a line. Teammates were supposed to have each other's backs. I knew some shit about guys I'd played hockey with over the years, and I wouldn't have dreamed of repeating any of it.

"Drink this," Boone said, passing me a shot as I walked back to our table in the bar.

"What is it?"

He lowered his brows. "Who cares? Just drink it."

I'd been nursing a single beer since we got here, because I wanted to be able to drive if Sariah picked up the phone. I shook my head at my teammate.

"You take it."

"Come on, we're celebrating. Drink it!"

"We won one game, douchebag. I don't want to be hungover tomorrow; there's still a lot of work to do."

"Whatever, grandpa." He clinked his shot glass against the one our teammate Kerry was holding, and tipped it back, making a face afterward. "Ah, Fireball. Hurts so good."

I took my phone from my pocket and checked it again. Nothing.

After last night, I knew where her apartment

was. Should I drive there and ask her if we could talk? I didn't think I could just stand here and smile like everything was fine.

"What crawled up your ass and died?" Drew asked me, walking over with a glass of ice water in hand.

"Have you heard if Alvarado is coming?"

He pinched his brows together in confusion. "No, but he usually never goes out after games. Why?"

"That cocksucker fucked me over tonight. When I see him, I'm gonna pull his nut sac out through his throat."

"Sounds entertaining. What'd he do?"

"Remember what I told you about Sariah? How I met her and all?"

"Yeah."

"I have no idea how he knew about it, but he told Sariah. The only people who know are you, me, and Lars."

"Shit." Drew rubbed his chin, looking thoughtful. "Do you think he was in the locker room that day you told me?"

I thought back to that day. Alvarado and I had just finished our bag skate punishment, so he easily could have still been in the locker room right after that. How could I have been so fucking stupid?

"That's possible," I admitted.

"Still an absolute dick move."

I ran my hand through my hair, exhaling hard. "I was planning to tell her. Not anytime soon, but honestly, I was. The lie just got out of hand as I got to know her better and liked her more and more."

"I heard you guys did the mattress mambo last night."

"Who said that?"

He shrugged. "Locker room talk."

"That locker room is like a fucking sorority house."

"Minus the hot chicks, you are correct, sir."

Rubbing the bridge of my nose, I weighed my options. It was going on midnight, but there was no way I'd be able to sleep anytime soon.

I'd deal with Alvarado later. What mattered now was getting through to Sariah. After checking my phone again and finding no texts, I shoved it in my pocket and pulled out my wallet.

"Pay our table's waitress for me, will you?" I said, pulling out two twenties.

Drew put up a hand. "I've got you. Put that money away. Where are you going?"

"To her place."

He widened his eyes. "Bro, I'm not sure that's a wise move."

"I'm not staying here and drinking beer with you asswipes and making her think I don't even care."

"Yeah, but…she just found out. Give her time to cool down."

"Does Nina need time to cool down when she's pissed?"

Drew laughed. "Yeah, dude. I've learned when to shut the fuck up."

"What woman doesn't want to hear that you know you fucked up and you're sorry?"

"Angry women aren't reasonable. They're like venomous snakes with their hoods up and their tongues sticking out at you. Fucking run, and chat up that snake later, when it's had a good meal and is coiled up and chilling."

"Think I should bring her some food?"

He shrugged. "Couldn't hurt. Might want to wear your hockey gear, too, in case she throws dishes at your head."

"Sariah's not like that."

My teammate arched his brows skeptically. "For your sake, I hope not. I'm just saying, better safe than nailed in the nuts with a serving fork."

———

"Nash?"

My back hit the floor as Sariah opened the door to her apartment the next morning, sunlight making me shield my eyes as I looked up at her.

"Sariah." I wiped a hand over my mouth to clear away the drool I felt there and jumped to my feet.

I remembered driving here last night and sending another dozen or so texts telling her I was at her door. Since she had neighbors and it was the middle of the night, I hadn't wanted to bang on her door and wake anyone up. Apparently I'd fallen asleep sitting on the ground outside her door.

And damn, was I feeling it. My left hip ached, I was thirsty as hell, and my suit looked like I'd…well, slept in it. Which I had.

"Were you sleeping outside my door?" she asked.

I ran a hand through my hair and found a leaf, which I plucked out and dropped to the ground. If Sariah would just let me in, we could have a cup of coffee and talk things out.

"Can I come in?"

She scoffed. "No. I'm leaving for work."

I looked down at my wristwatch. It was seven thirty a.m.

"We need to talk," I said. "Please."

"There's nothing to talk about. You're a liar and a

scam artist. Which is just weird, by the way. I have nothing to be scammed out of, and you're a millionaire."

"None of it happened on purpose."

She crossed her arms over her chest. "Oh, so it was just random. *Right*."

"It was. I swear."

"Your word means nothing to me. Now move. I need to get to work."

"Just give me ten minutes. Please. I'd give my left nut for some coffee from your Keurig and ten minutes of your time."

Her grip on the side of her door tightened, her knuckles whitening. "You have a lot of fucking nerve asking me to make you coffee after you lied to me. Get the hell out of here."

I took a step forward and she looked up at me, her hazel eyes swimming with emotion.

"I'm sorry. You have no idea how sorry I am it went down like this."

She looked away, her voice insistent. "Move."

"Can you just let me in for ten minutes?"

"You are not coming into my apartment." She stepped outside, forcing me to move out of the way, and used a key to lock her door.

"Why are you so adamant about me not coming

in?" My pulse pounded nervously. "Is there someone in there?"

She scowled. "Like it's any of your fucking business."

"Sariah." I put my hands on either side of her door near her shoulders, boxing her in. "I haven't even looked at another woman since we started texting. I was an asshole and I was wrong, but…if Eric Alvarado is in your apartment, I'm going to break down this door and then I'm going to break his goddamn face."

"Why would Alvarado be in my apartment?"

"He wanted to score points with you by being the one to tell you. That fucker has it out for me. And if he slept with the woman he knows I'm into, I will—"

"You're fucking serious." Sariah put a palm on my chest and pushed, but I didn't budge.

"Move, Nash."

I was irrational, practically shaking with anger. "Tell me the truth."

She shook her head. "Even now, it's about your ego, isn't it? Can't have Alvarado getting your piece, right?"

"You have never been that to me. Never. But he's taken things to a level he's not ready for."

Her gaze softened. "This isn't you, Nash. You're not a guy who forces a woman to stay somewhere she doesn't want to be or gets sent to jail for beating up teammates."

I dropped my hands from the door, shamed. "No, I'm not forcing you to do anything."

"I want to go to work now. I'm done with this conversation."

She turned and started walking away, and I followed.

"It was a coincidence, Sariah. I found out the day you started working for the Mavericks. When you told me your name, I figured it had to be you."

She picked up her pace, her heels clicking on the concrete sidewalk.

"But what would I have said?" I continued. "Right there in front of Kevin, you wanted me to ask if you were the same Sariah I'd been texting?"

She reached her sedan, and as she took the keys out of her bag, I noticed her hand was shaking.

"You could have texted me. Called me that night. You had so many opportunities to tell me, but instead you *used* me. And it worked, right? You got me in bed. Go high-five your teammates about what a player you are and move on to your next victim."

"I really like you," I said as she got into her car. "I was wrong and I'm sorry and I'll do whatever I need to so I can make things right."

"So you can continue sleeping with the woman

you scammed? Sounds pretty amazing. Fuck you, Nash."

She put her hand on the door handle and I saw my chance slipping away.

"I wanted you to know me," I said, the words coming out in a rush. "The real me. The guy who likes cereal and horror movies and hanging out with my dogs. I wanted you to like that guy. Not the hockey star or the rich guy or the guy with the abs in the underwear ad."

She narrowed her eyes. "I hate that underwear picture and you know it."

"You know what I'm saying. I made up the name Rob because I didn't know who you were and I had *no idea* what you were going to become to me. If I could do it over, I'd do it differently."

"The truth is, you're all those things you mentioned above. And you withheld that from me. It would be one thing if we hadn't slept together, but… fuck, Nash, you *hurt* me. So bad. And for your teammates to know and not me? For you to make me into a locker room joke?"

"I didn't—"

She cut me off. "You asked me to forgive you, and my answer is no. It's not a soft no, or a no laced with a maybe, it's a hard no. I'm done with you. Now leave me alone."

She pulled on her car door, forcing me to jump back to avoid having the door closed on me.

I watched as she drove away. She was almost out of the lot when I had to squint to see if...wait, was she flipping me off in her rearview mirror?

Yeah, she was. I was completely fucked.

CHAPTER TWENTY-THREE

Sariah

SWEAT POURED OFF ME LIKE A FREAKIN' faucet, but the physical labor felt better than emotional pain, so I was focusing on the former. Today was moving day, and I couldn't express how relieved I was to have two whole days off from the Mavericks. The team was out of town anyway, but not having to go into the office made it easier not to think about the clusterfuck my life had become. Because of a man.

Again.

I was going to join a convent if this shit kept up.

The moving truck hadn't arrived yet, but my parents and sisters were here. Sophia had dropped Revy off with her in-laws, so she and her husband had committed to being here all day, alone with Sami and Sebastian.

As predicted, Mom was putting away the groceries she'd thoughtfully picked up for me, and Sophia and Sami were wiping down every possible surface with disinfectant. Dee had just arrived with donuts and bagels and we put everything out in the kitchen since we'd be hungry as the day went on.

"Sariah, are you sure this is where you want the TV?" Dad called from the living room.

"That's the only place for it," I replied. "And I don't watch much TV anyway."

"Okay." He went back to whatever he was attaching to the wall to hang it from.

"You're awfully quiet," Dee murmured, following me when I went into the bathroom to hang the new shower curtain I'd treated myself to. It was Paris themed, with the Eiffel Tower surrounded by flowers and the words "Je t'aime." I didn't know who I loved at this point in my life, but the pink-and-black color scheme made me happy.

"Busy day," I responded.

I hadn't caught her up on things with Nash/Rob yet, and I wasn't going to get into it in the middle of moving.

"You're full of shit," she said, handing me the last two shower curtain hooks. "Something happen with that Rob guy? Oh my god! Did you meet up with him and not tell anyone?"

"I'll tell you later," I said, pulling the shower curtain closed and smiling at it. "There. That looks pretty."

"It does."

"Hey, Sariah, the movers are here!" Sami called out.

"Coming." I turned and headed toward the living room, shocked to see my mother carrying the biggest bouquet of pink roses I'd ever seen.

"Where did those come from?" I asked her.

"They're from Nash," Sophia said, waving a little white card at me. "Who's Nash and what is he apologizing for?"

I snatched the card from her hand. "Have you ever heard of privacy? Do I read your mail?"

She shrugged. "It's mostly bills, so you're welcome to."

"He's no one," I muttered, reading the note for myself.

Sariah—

I'm so sorry. I know you're still mad, but I didn't know how to tell you the truth. You have to believe me. Please give me another chance. I'll do anything you ask of me.

Nash

"WHOEVER HE IS," Sami said, reading over my shoulder. "Couldn't you have dumped him after he helped you move?"

"He's out of town," I said, crumpling up the note and tossing it into the trash can in the kitchen.

Luckily, no one in the family seemed to put the name Nash together with the Nash Reilly from the Mavericks, but Dee did. There was a slight crease between her eyes as she drew her brows together, but I didn't dare make eye contact. She could read me like a book and I didn't have time for that today.

"They're coming up with your bed," Dad said. "Make sure you tell them where you want it."

I wanted to laugh since the bedroom was small and there was really only one wall that would work.

"Once your dresser is up here, I'll start putting away your clothes," Dee said.

"Thanks." I smiled at her and headed into the hallway to direct the movers. Sebastian and Felipe were also helping out since Sebastian's friend ran the moving company. With two extra sets of hands, they would finish faster, which meant it would cost me less money. My family drove me crazy sometimes, but I was eternally grateful to have them. Otherwise, it probably would have been just me and Dee today, which was laughable. It would have taken us three years to get everything up the stairs.

"Whoever Nash is—" Sami said, trailing off to scowl down at the lamp she was carrying awkwardly in her arms. "I hope you don't forgive him because if you get back together after we finish moving you in without his help, I'm going to give him a piece of my mind."

I sighed. "We are definitely not getting back together."

"How did no one know you were dating someone?" Mom asked. "And where did you meet him? Is he attractive?"

"Doesn't matter." I slid my feet into my sneakers.

"Those were some pretty expensive roses," Mom said, taking a box from Sebastian. "Does he have money?"

"We're not talking about this," I said, going out the front door and heading for the stairs.

I didn't know for sure how Nash had gotten my new address, but I was going to have to have a chat with Mo when she got back to town.

IT WAS late when everyone left, close to nine o'clock. But I was moved in. My clothes were put away, Mom and Sophia had unpacked and organized the kitchen, I'd put toiletries and miscellaneous items in the bathroom, and the guys made sure all my appliances and electronics were working. Basic cable was included with the rent, so they'd hooked everything up, and the cable guy was coming on Tuesday with a box so I could upgrade to get more channels. Dee and I had put fresh linens on my bed and now she was putting away a box of books.

"Dee, it's late," I called to her. "Come relax."

"I know you're going to be working crazy hours starting Monday," she said. "Which means the boxes that are left unpacked will sit here until your next vacation."

I chuckled. "Maybe, but you've done more than enough. Let's crack open that bottle of wine you brought over."

"Oooh. Wine." Her blue eyes sparkled with mischief. "I like wine. Do you know where your mom put your corkscrew?"

"I threw it out," I told her. "Instead, I kept Theo's fancy automatic wine opener. It's in the cabinet to the left of the fridge."

Dee opened the bottle of Riesling she'd brought over while I got two wine glasses down. My mom and sisters were nosy as hell, but they'd done a great job in the kitchen.

"So." Dee sank down on the couch, wine glass in hand. "Are you going to tell me about Nash?"

I sighed. "It's a long story and I'm tired."

"Then tell me what happened with Rob."

I leaned back against the cushions. "Rob and Nash are the same person."

The play of emotions on Dee's face would have been comical had it not been so heartbreaking. She went from confusion to horror to fury.

"Are you fucking kidding me? Nash Reilly was catfishing you by pretending to be someone else?"

"To be fair," I said quickly. "I'm the one who dialed his number by mistake. So it's not like he sought me out. It was a coincidence that the guy I dialed by mistake turned out to be one of the Mavericks. And he didn't know right away either. It wasn't until I started working there that he put two and two together."

"And he didn't tell you?"

"Nope."

"But it's not like you guys were involved, so why would he keep it a secret?"

"We slept together," I said, taking a big gulp of wine.

"You slept with Nash Reilly?" Her eyes were so

wide I was afraid she was going to hurt herself. "Seriously? And you didn't tell me?"

"It just happened the other day and then…" I downed the rest of my wine. "Then shit hit the fan."

"I'm confused. I think you need to start at the beginning."

"I better get the bottle," I said, getting up.

"And some cheese and crackers," she said, getting up and following me. "I worked hard today. And that Chinese food we ordered didn't fill me up."

We finished the Riesling and opened a bottle of prosecco next. We were both pretty tipsy by the time I'd filled her in on what had been going on the last month or so and she giggled.

"I want to be mad you kept all this from me, but I'm still trying to process the fact that you slept with Nash Reilly. I mean, shitty personality aside, he's fucking beautiful. Please don't tell me he's selfish in bed."

I groaned. "No. Not even a little. Best sex of my life."

"Why are the best lovers the biggest jerks?" she asked sadly. "Damn, I hate this for you. But I also hate this Eric guy. I mean, what a dick move to tell you. I bet he never gets invited to another team BBQ. Wonder what Nash did to make him want to get revenge like this."

"What do you mean?" I asked in confusion.

"What do you mean what do I mean?" She cocked her head. "You don't think Eric did this out of the kindness of his heart, do you? He wouldn't betray his teammate unless he either has a thing for you or Nash pissed him off and he wanted to get him back."

I stared at her. "I hadn't even considered that. I was so pissed at Nash, I just thought he was being a nice guy. Shit. And he's married, so I'm pretty sure he doesn't have a thing for me. I don't think we've said ten words to each other since I started working there."

"Mark my words—there's friction between him and Nash."

"Yeah, now that I think about it, Nash mentioned that Eric was kind of a dick. They'd gone back and forth with some hazing and practical jokes, but I just thought it was typical locker room stuff. It didn't occur to me there was actual beef there. I don't think there was on Nash's part. He and Lars and Boone are always busting each other's balls, so this feels different."

Dee's eyelids were starting to droop. "Did you like him? I mean, really like him?"

"Who? Nash or Rob?"

"They're the same person. If you liked one, you liked the other."

"I had a strong emotional connection with one, and a strong physical attraction to the other."

"They're the *same* person." She glared at me. "And you didn't answer my question."

"Well, yeah, of course I liked them. Him. Whatever. But it doesn't matter. That ship has sailed. He used me."

"How?"

"What?"

"How did he use you? You texted him first. You yourself admit it was a coincidence that your wrong text went to someone on the Mavericks. By that time, you guys were friends. Then he met you, and even though you didn't know it was him, you liked Nash. You also said you were looking to let your hair down that night you hooked up, so you were interested in sleeping with him. If you'd said no, he wouldn't have forced the issue."

"Of course not. Nash would never…" My voice trailed off. The last thing I wanted to do was defend the lying bastard.

"So explain how he used you?"

"Fine. He didn't use me—he scammed me and let me believe he was someone he wasn't!"

"Not really. Nash was always just Nash. And when he realized there was no good way to tell you the truth, he basically had Rob ghost you."

"Whose side are you on?"

"Yours, girlfriend. Always. Which is why I need to play devil's advocate once in a while to make you look at the whole picture."

"It doesn't matter," I said sharply. "He should have come clean the moment he realized who I was."

"Yes, he should have."

"But?"

"But maybe he was afraid just like you were. Maybe he was tired of girls who were after his money, his looks, whatever. Maybe—"

"Enough." I held up a hand. "I love you and you've been incredible today, but I don't want to talk about Nash anymore. It's done. So let's drop it."

"No regrets?"

"Nope."

Well, maybe a little tiny bit of regret.

But I'd never say that out loud.

CHAPTER TWENTY-FOUR

Nash

"Who gives a shit that we lost last night? This really puts things into perspective," Wes said, shaking his head.

We were standing outside the funeral home where Annie's funeral service had just been held, waiting for Lars to pick us up in his SUV so we could all ride to the cemetery together.

Sawyer had asked me, Wes, Lars, and Drew to be pallbearers. I'd been surprised and deeply honored by the request. Almost everyone from the Mavericks organization had been at the funeral service, and I'd seen Sariah and felt her gaze on me as we carried Annie's casket out, but it wasn't the right time to engage with her.

Damn, did I want to, though. I saw her standing with some other front office people about a hundred feet away, looking beautiful in formfitting black slacks and a dark-gray short-sleeved blouse, her hair pulled back in a neat bun, and it was all I could do not to walk over there, take her hand and beg her forgiveness.

Sawyer had eulogized his wife at her funeral service. He'd wiped the corners of his eyes, smiled sadly and started by saying, "I was told spouses don't usually do this, but Annie and I never played by any other rules but our own, so I'm not following that one, either."

He'd tearfully told everyone the story of how he and Annie met, about feeling like he'd been struck by lightning the day he met his future wife.

"Annie used to say finding true love was like calling the IRS and having a real, live person pick up on the first ring," he'd said, his voice thick with emotion. "Like getting to Hannah's Kitchen, our favorite bakery, after seven in the morning and still getting a hot and fresh frosted cinnamon roll. What are the chances?"

His words were still ringing in my ears. What were the chances a woman who lives in the same city as me would accidentally text me and end up taking me completely by storm? That she'd end up working for my team? That she'd be not just beautiful, but smart, strong, and funny as hell?

It was so unlikely and yet…here we were. It had to mean something that fate had brought Sariah and I together, and I knew it wasn't supposed to end like this.

Lars pulled up nearby and Wes, Drew, and I loaded into his vehicle and we drove over to the ceremony for the burial. Tomorrow morning, the team was flying to Detroit for our third playoff game, but today, that was the furthest thing from anyone's mind. Wes was right. It was hard to get worked up over a game when you watched a family grieving the loss of their beautiful daughter, sister, aunt, wife, and friend. She was so young.

"I can't believe we're doing this again," Wes said softly from the back seat. "Doesn't it seem like yesterday we were burying Ben and Lauren?"

"In some ways it does," I said. "In other ways it feels like forever."

"I miss him," Drew said as Lars drove. "He would've been on fire over that loss last night."

I met his gaze in the rearview mirror, smiling. "I was thinking that same thing when Wes was talking to the ref about that knee to knee they missed. Ben would've had a hard time letting that go."

"Remember that time he asked a ref if it was his

first night on the job?" Wes said. "And then it turned out it was."

We all laughed at the memory. It was getting easier to laugh and smile when we thought of him. For a while, it had just been painful. I had only been able to think of his two young children, and the knowledge that Ben and Lauren's son would have no conscious memories of his parents.

"He'd tell us to get our heads out of our asses in Detroit," Wes said. "I can practically hear him telling me to get out of my own way."

"He used to tell me that, too," Drew said.

After about a minute of silence, Wes said, "Nash, Drew told me about what Alvarado did. It was shitty of him, and I appreciate you not saying anything to him at the service."

I turned and glared at him. "Come on, I'm not that big of an asshole. That wasn't the time or the place."

"Agreed, and neither is Detroit."

I scoffed. "It might be."

"It's not. We've just barely gotten our shit together as a team again and we're in the playoffs. This has been a long time coming. The last thing we need is bad press or fighting in the locker room."

"I'm not acting like it didn't happen."

"I'm not asking you to. I'm asking you to wait."

"Alvarado's on the third line," I said. "You think him playing with a black eye or a cracked jaw is going to matter?"

"Jesus, Nash, are you new here? I think washing my fucking socks is going to mess with my mojo, so I've been wearing the same smelly ones I had on during the semis."

Hockey players were superstitious. I always had pasta on game days, and I practiced the same routines for stretching and taping my game sticks. But this shit with Alvarado was not that.

"You know what messed with my mojo?" I asked Wes. "When Alvarado fucked me over and told Sariah I'm an opportunistic asshole who was trying to game her."

"Were you?"

"Fuck no," I said indignantly. "How can you even ask me that?"

"I'm just trying to figure out what prompted you to keep a secret like that from her."

"It's a long story."

"Summarize it," Wes said.

I turned around to glare at him, sitting in the back seat. "I wanted to see how she felt about me without knowing about the fame and the money."

"Why, bro?" Drew quipped. "Those are literally your only redeeming qualities."

I ignored the jab and continued. "After I didn't tell her the truth on the day I found out I was texting her, every day after that felt like it was too late. Like she'd wonder why I waited so long to confess."

"I get it," Wes said. "And Alvarez will get his, I promise you that."

I sighed heavily. "I don't want this to spread around the locker room. It's embarrassing for Sariah. Can we keep it to just the people in this car?"

"Of course," Wes said. "But I can't control what Alvarado says."

Lars shrugged. "By the time Nash and I are through with him, he won't want to say anything."

"After the season, okay?" Wes practically begged. "I'm stressed enough already, and I don't need it leaking that we've got a feud going on. Especially now. We need to be united behind Sawyer right now."

"And later we can unite behind punishing Alvarado?" Lars asked.

"We can," Wes confirmed.

I wanted to respect his wishes, but I didn't think I could wait that long.

———

I MET Sariah's eyes as Sawyer wept, his hand on his wife's casket. It was time to lower it into the ground, and he couldn't seem to bring himself to let her go. Sariah wiped at the corners of her eyes, and I did the same.

The feelings surging through me were painful. Did I want to love a woman as much as Sawyer loved Annie? Did I want to risk my whole world crumbling around me because something I had no control over had happened?

The alternative was to play it safe. Stick to casual hookups. Have close friends and have lovers, but never let them be one and the same. I'd been doing that for a while now, and doing pretty damn well at it.

Wes stepped forward and put his hand on Sawyer's shoulder. Sawyer nodded and let his hand slide off of the casket. Putting an arm around his shoulder, Wes walked him the few steps back to his mom, who wrapped both arms around her son as he silently cried.

Wes walked back to where Hadley was standing. She looked somber in a black short-sleeved dress, her hair around her shoulders. She reached up and wiped a tear from the corner of Wes's eye, and he leaned his forehead against hers. When she slid her hand around to the back of his neck and mouthed "I love you" to him, I knew.

I wanted it.

Sawyer was right—real love was rare. It was also messy and painful and, at times, all-consuming. But life without it was like living in black and white. Sariah was my chance to live life every day in vivid color, and I wanted it. I couldn't say for sure that I was in love with her, but I knew the potential was there.

I looked away from Wes and Hadley, clearing the lump from my throat, while searching out Sariah. There she was. Looking right back at me.

What was she thinking? I knew she was pissed and had every right to be, but was she also feeling something—anything—else?

The service ended and those of us who weren't in Annie's immediate family headed for our own cars. When I turned to look over my shoulder, I saw Sawyer kneeling on the ground next to his wife's burial plot.

I never wanted to hurt like that, but I knew that hurting the way he was right now was part of loving a woman as much as he loved Annie.

Rosa Romano, the owner of our team, hosted lunch for everyone at a local restaurant. The entire time, I was either glaring at Alvarado or staring at

Sariah; there had to be a way for us to move forward.

Wes walked over and put a hand on my shoulder, leaning down to speak near my ear. "Sawyer asked a few of us to stop by the house."

I nodded and got up immediately, even though I was only halfway done with my food. Sawyer's family had planned to gather at his house after the service, and we hadn't wanted to intrude on that so we'd come to the team lunch instead. But if my teammate wanted anything from me today, it was his.

On my way out of the restaurant, I buttoned my suit jacket and gave Sariah a final longing gaze, remembering the one and only night of passion and intimacy we'd shared.

I was determined for us to have more than that one night together, though. A hell of a lot more.

CHAPTER TWENTY-FIVE

Sariah

IT HAD BEEN a long week since Annie died. Between the breakup with Nash, moving, Annie's death and funeral, and then losing three in a row to Detroit, I was emotionally exhausted. Tonight was game five, finally back here at home, and the team had to pull out a win or the season was over. They'd played hard, but it was obvious the fire they'd had before Annie's death had dimmed. And not just a little.

I wasn't an athlete, so I had no idea how you pulled up your britches and played through something like this, but I imagined it was terrible. From what I'd heard, several of the wives had been very close to Annie, and their husbands by extension. The funeral had been one of the saddest events I'd ever attended, and I hadn't even known her.

When my phone rang, I picked it up on autopilot. "This is Sariah. How can I help you?"

"Hey, Sariah. It's Everett."

"Hi. How are you?"

"How are you? I heard about one of your players' wives passing away and the funeral was all over the local news."

"Yeah, it's been a rough week."

"You can see it in their playing."

"Are you pulling your ads?"

There was a pause. "Seriously? Is that what you think of me? When have I ever been so obsessed with money that it came before compassion?"

"I'm sorry." I rubbed my pointer and middle fingers back and forth across my forehead, hoping it would alleviate the tension there. "The last week has been…hard."

"I'm sure. And no, I'm not pulling my ads. I wanted to get seats to the game. We were supposed to be in Florida with my in-laws, but Cora has a dance recital this afternoon so we had to cancel. I don't miss my baby girl's performances if I can help it. But this means we can come to the game tonight."

"I'll comp you two tickets," I said, opening my email so I could request them from Lance. Everett had become a big spender the last couple of months, so it wouldn't be a problem. "They'll be at the will call window."

"You don't have to do that."

"I know. But I want to. And sorry I'm cranky."

"You're allowed. Listen, once the season is over, we're going to have you over to the house. Cora wants to show you her new bedroom furniture."

I smiled. Everett's six-year-old daughter was adorable and the last time I'd been at the house, I'd gotten sucked into hours of Candy Land games and nail painting, while the rest of the guests had been out back drinking and having grown-up conversations. When Everett had realized I was missing, he'd come looking for me and found Cora and me laughing hysterically at the mess we'd made of our nails. I was pretty sure that one evening had solidified him as a customer of mine forever.

"I'm in," I said.

"Okay, great. Will I see you tonight?"

"I'll come find you between periods."

"See you later."

I disconnected just as Mo came over to me carrying a large manila envelope.

"What's that?" I asked.

"Divorce papers," she said quietly. "Tony's not going to contest anything. We're splitting all marital assets down the middle. I keep my car, he keeps his truck. We both keep our retirement accounts. House goes on the market this week and we'll split the profit."

"Oh, hon, I'm sorry." I looked up at her. "At least it sounds very fair. Are you okay with those numbers and all the emotional aspects of it?"

"I'm shell-shocked but hanging in there. I'm just glad it's going to be amicable. I was afraid he'd fight me on everything. He's been such a dick the last month or so."

"He knows better because that lawyer Lars found for you sounds badass."

"She totally is." Mo smiled. "I'm really grateful for the friends I have here with the Mavericks. That lawyer saved my ass. Or at least my state of mind. Same thing."

We both chuckled.

"Anyway, wanna go to lunch?" she asked. "I feel like Italian…something decadent and fattening and comforting."

I shook my head. "Honestly, the food sounds good, but I just want to bury myself in work and not think about all the shitty things happening in the world."

She sighed. "I hear that. But sometimes friendship and laughter can be the best medicine."

"I know. Just…not today."

"Okay. Should we order in then?"

"Sure." I waved a hand. "I'll eat anything when it comes to Italian food. Just get me something from wherever you choose."

She eyed me. "You sure you're okay? You are not yourself and it's starting to freak me out."

I shrugged. "I feel guilty even talking about my situation, considering what happened to Annie, but that doesn't mean it doesn't exist or that it doesn't hurt."

Her face softened and she dropped her voice. "Nash." She knew the whole story and though she'd been sympathetic and supportive, she'd also been of the mindset that Nash was a good guy who'd simply made a mistake. According to Mo, he was miserable too, but I wasn't sure how to reconcile how much I missed him with how angry I was that he'd deceived me.

"I don't expect you to take sides," I said quietly. "I know you've been friends with him a lot longer than you have with me and—"

"Stop it." She shook her head. "It's not about sides. I let him know what a numbskull he is in no uncertain terms. I let him have it—you would have loved it."

I managed a tiny smile.

"But in the grand scheme of things, what did he do that was so bad? He didn't take anything from you. Rob was basically an online friend. You talked, you laughed, you confided in each other. But there was no depth there. Nash is real. He's here for you. He brings you coffee every damn day. He's shown you the sweet, kind man beneath the rough-around-the-edges exterior. I know he rocked your world between the sheets. And that matters. I could sleep through Tony's lovemaking."

I grimaced. "That's awful. I don't think I've ever had a lover *that* boring. A little boring, but not sleepworthy."

"You don't have to talk to me about what you're thinking right now—I know it's been a rough week on all fronts. Just think about it. Think about what you might be letting go over what amounts to a bad judgment call. Because we all make mistakes."

I loved Mo, but this was so frustrating. Why was everyone so quick to forgive him? Was I the asshole in this situation?

She nodded when I didn't respond. "Okay, I'm going to order Italian. I'll let you know when it gets here." She patted my shoulder and headed off toward her office.

I stared after her for a few seconds, trying to pull my psyche out of the deepest, darkest parts of my soul. The parts that mourned the death of a woman I hadn't known. The parts that wanted the team to make a comeback tonight so badly, but I had a feeling they might not. The part that had been bruised and emotionally battered by an ex who cheated and therefore refused to make excuses for anyone who lied in any way. The part that still ached for Nash even though he'd hurt me.

Ugh. I put my head in my hands and tried to breathe.

How had everything gone so wrong in such a short amount of time?

"Hey, uh, Sariah?"

The voice made me jump and I lifted my head, shocked to see Eric standing there. He was on my shit list too, because after talking to Dee about the whole thing, I realized that he hadn't told me about Nash for any altruistic reasons and I detested being a pawn in whatever bullshit he and Nash had going on. It was almost as bad as what Nash had done.

"What can I do for you?" I asked in what I hoped was my most professional, neutral voice.

"Could we talk somewhere private for a second?"

I eyed him. "I don't think we have anything to say to each other. Do you have more locker room gossip to share with me?"

He swallowed hard, his Adam's apple bobbing nervously. "I, uh, I just need a minute."

"Say what you have to say." There was only one other guy in the general area at the moment, and he was on the phone, so I figured we'd just get this over with.

"I wanted to apologize."

"Oh, really?"

"What I did was totally uncalled for, and honestly, none of my business. I was snooping because…I was mad at Nash and I have a bunch of my own shit going on. But I shouldn't have gotten involved. It wasn't fair to him and it definitely wasn't fair to you. I didn't realize…" His voice trailed off and he looked away.

I wasn't going to make this easy for him, so I just waited.

"I didn't realize he really cares about you."

"How do you even know that?" I demanded.

"I hear things. I see how down he's been since everything happened. I didn't know you two were, you know, involved. Like a relationship."

I almost denied it but opted not to give him more information than he already had. So I kept my mouth shut, waiting for him to say whatever he needed to say.

"Anyway, I'm sorry I messed things up between

you both and I hope you can eventually forgive me. And him. More him than me. I don't know the details of what went on, but I know he's been pretty gutted since it all went down."

"Is that true or are you just covering your ass because the whole team is pissed at you?" I asked quietly.

He shook his head. "As far as I know, he didn't tell anybody but Lars, Drew, and Wes. Everyone except them has been the same to me. I'm sure I'll get what's coming to me after the season is over. But this is about doing what's right. Some fucked-up shit has gone on in my life and I realized that I put some of it on you and Nash, which wasn't cool. I don't know if I can undo the damage I did, but I wanted you to know the other side to things."

"I appreciate that."

"So, uh, yeah. That's it. Take care." He turned and started walking away.

"Hey, Eric?" I called out to him.

"Yeah?" He looked back at me.

"Good luck tonight."

CHAPTER TWENTY-SIX

Nash

THE FANS HAD QUIETED.

It happened in the blink of an eye, as the die-hard fans looked at the clock and realized a victory was mathematically impossible. We'd known it would be an uphill battle coming into this period down by three goals, but now we were in the final minute of the game, and only the Detroit fans were cheering.

They'd scored on us again in this period, and their goaltender was almost supernatural in his ability to sense when and where every shot was coming from.

Final score: 5–1 Detroit. *Fuck.*

There was speculation that Annie Cain's death

had rattled our mojo and we'd never gotten it back. I didn't think that was the case. Detroit had just been hungrier for it than we were.

And also, though I'd never say it out loud, Drew's goaltending had been a big contributor to the games we'd lost, especially on the road. He'd been considering retiring, and I had a feeling he'd be making a graceful exit in the off-season to avoid being forced out.

Hell of a way for a future Hall of Famer to go out, but that was professional sports.

"I'm so sorry, guys," Drew said. We were all back in the locker room after the game.

"You've got nothing to apologize for," Wes said, his expression defeated. "Our problem was scoring one fucking goal over three periods."

It was one thing to lose—that happened to every team on a regular basis—but getting the shit kicked out of you, on your home ice, while your loved ones and the fans watched? That fucking hurt. There was no way around it. We were collectively angry and sad, of course, but mostly we felt like a dejected bunch of failures.

Some of these guys had to go face their wives and kids tonight. Probably tomorrow for some of the kids, because it was late. And hell, who wanted to deal with a cranky kid in a shitty diaper after a season-ending championship loss? Cringe.

I'd always thought that would suck, to have a wife asking you if you were okay after a loss. The answer was always no. But I had a feeling Sariah wasn't the type to ask if I was okay. And it wouldn't have been the worst thing to have her waiting for me after the game, offering to either help me drown my sorrows or fuck them away.

With her, I'd definitely choose the second option. Not that it was even on the table. I'd blown things with her.

There was only one upside to the season ending tonight. I'd told Wes I wouldn't confront Alvarado over what he'd done until the season was over. Well, the season was now over and when he walked back into the main locker room area after his shower, I was waiting.

"Is there some reason you decided to fuck up my life?" I asked him. "Or are you just a spiteful little bitch who can't stand to see other people happy?"

He sighed heavily. "I'm sorry, man."

"That's it? That's all you have to say?"

He looked from side to side. "Can we talk about this somewhere else?"

"You want to come back to my place?" I scoffed.

"Maybe curl up in front of the fire with a glass of wine?"

He lowered his voice, his expression weary. "Like I told Sariah, it was more about me than you. I've got some shit going on in my own life, and that day I took things out on the closest target, which was you. It's not like you haven't been dicking with me every chance you get, and I wanted payback. But I admit, it was wrong and completely fucked up."

"Wait. You talked to Sariah? When?"

"Earlier today."

Hope surged within me. "What did she say?"

"Not much. I did the best I could to let her know you're not the jackass I made you out to be that day."

Well, shit. I'd been hoping I'd get to pound on his face a little bit. Now I'd look like an asshole if I did. I didn't forgive Alvarado, and I still didn't like him—not even a little bit—but he looked beaten in every way and I had a thing against kicking people when they were down.

"I gave you shit because it's what veterans do to rookies," I said.

He nodded. "I know. I could've handled it better."

"Jesus, you two." One of our defenders, Shane McManus, was glowering. "Our season just ended and I'm watching a live episode of the *Dr. Phil* show. Get a fucking room."

I glared at Alvarado. "This isn't over. And if she never forgives me, it'll never be over."

"Whatever, man," he mumbled.

I couldn't help feeling a little sorry for him. Whatever was going on, he looked wrecked. Or maybe it was just tonight's loss. Either way, I wasn't going to waste time worrying about the rookie who had fucked everything up with Sariah and me.

Dr. Phil would have told me *I* was the one who fucked everything up. And he wouldn't be wrong. I could admit to digging the hole I was now in, but how the hell was I going to get out of it?

ATHENA, Louie, and Archie were waiting by the front door when I walked inside my house later that night. Athena was first in line for attention. I rubbed her ears and tossed my car keys on the counter.

"You guys are lucky you missed that shit show of a game," I said. "You probably could've played better than we did."

It was about to be the end of an era. Drew had been the Mavericks starting goaltender for seven years now. This year had been our only shot to win a championship with all the key players who had been on the team when we lost Ben. I knew hockey, and

Drew, well enough to know that an announcement about his retirement would be coming within a few days.

"You guys want some bacon?" I asked the dogs.

Each dog began to wiggle in anticipation. They knew what the word *bacon* meant. I usually made them a couple pieces of bacon each when I returned from a road trip. Tonight I planned to eat some, too. I needed some comfort food, good ol' bacon and eggs.

I had several strips in a skillet and they were just starting to crackle when my phone rang. It was almost midnight and I wondered who would be calling me this late.

When I looked at the phone screen and saw Sariah's name, I picked it up and answered the call immediately, not caring about the bacon grease on my hands.

"Hello?"

There was a moment of silence before she said, "Hi."

"Hey. How are you?"

"I'm okay. I just wanted to say sorry you guys lost tonight."

I chuckled. "We didn't just lose; we got annihilated on our home ice. Thanks, though. It's nice to hear your voice."

I realized she wasn't likely to say "you, too" and after an awkward pause, she asked, "Were you ever going to tell me?"

"I was." I leaned back against my kitchen island. "I thought about it all the time. I wanted to wait until we were really solid and then take you out for a nice dinner and tell you right after we'd eaten our entrées, but before dessert."

She let out a single note of laughter. "That's weirdly specific."

"I didn't want it to be while you were hungry. No one likes to be surprised when they're waiting for their food to arrive. So I figured I'd take you to Carmine's, wine and dine you with a robust red and a nice steak. Then we'd order dessert and I'd put all my cards on the table while waiting for dessert to arrive."

"Because I wouldn't want to leave without eating dessert?" She laughed. "Are you serious right now?"

"It was the best I could come up with." I used a spatula to move the bacon around in the skillet. "I'm not used to apologizing to women."

"I can tell. Do you usually just try to make the woman feel like *she's* the one who was wrong? They teach that in Y-chromosome school, right? Along with how to leave the toilet seat up, piss on the floor, and lie well?"

"Ouch. There's a lot to unpack there."

"Okay, let's hear it, Nash. Or should I call you Rob?"

I groaned. "I'm sorry. I'll apologize every time you say the name Rob if you want. Say it a thousand times and I'll apologize a thousand times."

"It's not so much the words I want to hear. It's your explanation."

I turned down the burner on the stove, my dogs all sitting in front of the stove with expectant looks. We couldn't have burned bacon. I had the cooking time and temperature down to a science and they knew it.

"The truth is, in the past, when I've reached a point where I've fucked up with a woman and need to apologize, it's usually because I just don't care that much anymore about that casual relationship or where it's going. I'm over it, so I stop calling every day. Does that make sense? And then we decide to end things because she has expectations I'm unwilling to meet."

"Have you ever cheated in those situations?"

"No. I'd never cheat. Never."

She sighs. "I can't even tell you how shocked I was, Nash."

"I get that, and I'm so sorry you found out that way. I want you to know that you're different. I'm not over it—not even close. I don't want things to end. Whatever your expectations are, I want to meet them."

Archie gave a little whine, anxious for the bacon to finish cooking.

"Which one was that?" Sariah asked.

"Archie. I'm making bacon and it's smelling pretty damn good."

"For the dogs?"

"For all of us. I always eat after games."

She groaned. "You love those dogs so much and I can't lie. It's sexy."

My heart leaped hopefully. "I also give great oral, as you know."

"You do." She exhaled into the phone. "I don't know if I can forgive you. But I can't stop thinking about your parents' anniversary party coming up, and how I said I'd go with you."

An entire weekend to get back in her good graces was exactly what I needed. I hadn't planned to go for sure, but if it would help build up any trust with Sariah then I'd go.

"Will you still go?" I asked her, not breathing as I waited for her answer.

She took her sweet time answering, letting me sweat, but she finally said, "I will. But we're not sleeping together. We'll be staying in separate rooms.

I meant it when I said I don't know if I can forgive you."

"I understand."

"Before I go, can I ask you about something random?"

"Anything."

"I brought some playoff shirts and hats to the family suite tonight at the game and Drew's wife, Nina, looked heartbroken. Have you heard if anything is going on with her? I felt so bad. I kind of wanted to go give her a hug but I've never even spoken to her, so I ended up leaving."

Her kindness hit me from every direction.

"Was it toward the end of the game?" I asked.

"Yeah. When we knew the chances of winning were slim and we wanted to make sure everyone had gotten the playoff gear they wanted."

"This stays between you and me, okay?"

"Of course," she promised.

"She probably knew it was Drew's last game ever. I haven't heard anything for sure, but I imagine he's going to retire."

"Oh," she said softly. "Then yeah, that makes total sense."

"And it's not how he wanted to go out."

"Right." She paused. "I hope you and the dogs enjoy your bacon."

"Thanks. I'll text you our travel plans for the party."

"Okay, thanks. Can you also let me know how formal the party is going to be so I can pack the right clothes?"

"You got it."

"Thanks, Rob."

I grinned, amused by her sarcasm and her fire. "I'm sorry."

"Good night."

"Night, Sariah."

CHAPTER TWENTY-SEVEN

Sariah

Nash picked me up early the following Saturday morning. I'd originally said I would meet him at the airport, but that was my stubbornness costing me money. There was no reason for me to drive to the airport and park for the weekend, or even take an Uber both ways, simply because I didn't want Nash to think I'd forgiven him. Hell, I was going to have to spend the weekend with him, so if I'd agreed to go, I needed to behave like an adult. An adult who hadn't had her heart stomped on.

Again.

"There have to be some ground rules," I told him once we were settled in first class and had taken off.

"I thought we'd already covered that?" he asked, turning bright-blue eyes to me in confusion. "You have your own room at the hotel."

"Yes, but there's also the issue of who I am to you. You've obviously flown me out here to attend a very personal family event with you. They're going to assume I'm your girlfriend."

Nash didn't respond, merely watched me, waiting for me to continue.

"And I'm not."

"I'm aware."

I blew out an exasperated breath. "So what are you going to tell them?"

His eyes met mine and he waited another beat before saying, "What do you want me to tell them?"

He had me there.

Because I had no answer.

I definitely wasn't his girlfriend. I also wasn't some puck bunny he was screwing. And at this very moment, we weren't even friends. We couldn't tell people that, though. He had enough stress with this party and the situation with his dad. My job here wasn't to hurt him. At home, I'd make him pay for what he'd done. Probably for a long time. But this was different and no matter how angry I still was, my heart ached for him with regard to what his dad was doing to his mom.

"Let's just say we're good friends," I said at last.

"People will assume we're sleeping together."

Part of me wanted to screech in protest, but I reminded myself that this weekend, this party, this series of events that could potentially unfold, were not about me. "That's fine," I said, shrugging. "We are *not* going to encourage it, though. We're friends, we work together, that's all."

"Okay." He paused. "Is that it?"

God, he was infuriating sometimes.

"Yes." I looked up gratefully as the flight attendant brought us mimosas.

"Do you think you'll ever forgive me, Sariah?" he asked as we sipped our drinks.

"I don't know," I admitted, twirling my glass in my hand. "You know what I went through with Theo. I don't like liars. In fact, I despise liars."

"I could counter that it was more a lie of omission," he said. "But I'm guessing that distinction doesn't matter to you."

"No, it doesn't. It's almost worse because it means you knew better and continued to perpetuate the lie."

He sighed. "I'm crazy about you, Sariah. I don't know if I'll be able to show you how much this weekend. My gut tells me it's going to be a shit show.

But I need you to know that I wouldn't have asked you to come if you didn't mean a lot to me."

Somehow, I knew that, even if I wasn't ready to admit it.

"My mom is going to love you," he continued quietly. "Please don't make me look like a douche to her. She's going to have enough to deal with."

"I would never—" I began, but then cut myself off. "Wait, what do you mean? Are you going to tell her about your dad?"

He looked away and was quiet for a long time. "I'm caught between a rock and a hard place, Sariah. If I don't tell her, and let her enjoy the party as if her marriage is intact, isn't that perpetuating the same type of lie as I did with you?" He turned to look at me, and maybe for the first time in my life, I was speechless.

I hadn't made the correlation between the two situations, and it was jarring. He was in a terrible position.

"But if I tell her, it's going to ruin not just the party, but her entire life. How do I make that choice, babe?" His voice was soft and his hand shook a little as he lifted his glass, downing the rest of his mimosa.

If he'd said almost anything else, I would have told him not to call me "babe," but there was no doubt he was struggling, and I couldn't bring myself to be a bitch when it came to this situation.

"I don't know," I replied gently, putting my hand on his forearm. "In our case, it was wrong to keep the truth from me, and it probably is in your mom's case too, but it's a totally different thing. You and I had been together once. We're talking thirty years of marriage, family, memories, a lifetime for your mom. It's way more complicated."

"I don't know what to do."

"I don't either." I squeezed his arm. "But I'm here for you. As much as you piss me off, I'm here for you."

He laid his hand over mine for a moment and the warmth went right to my chest.

I could deny it all I wanted, but his touch did things to me.

Still.

———

My room at the Biltmore was gorgeous and I was almost sorry I had to leave it to go to the party. Nash had told me the dress code wasn't black tie, but formal, so he was wearing a suit and I had on a red cocktail dress that was formfitting and elegant. It was strapless but fell to midcalf and made me look long and lean. I'd actually never worn it before. I'd bought it for Theo's company Christmas party last year but then he'd come home with an obnoxious little black number and at the time I'd felt guilty saying no to his thoughtfulness even though the black dress was ugly. I'd donated it to charity the day he moved out.

Tonight I felt beautiful and classy.

When I opened the door to Nash, I knew he thought so too because those beautiful blue eyes of his darkened and narrowed slightly, raking me up and down without shame.

"I'm sorry," he said, when he caught my look. "But you're absolutely breathtaking. I…Jesus, Sariah, you're without a doubt the most beautiful woman I know and every man in the room is going to wonder what kind of idiot I am for not wanting something more with you."

"No one said you don't want more," I said coyly. "I'm just not on board."

He chuckled. "Touché. Are you ready?"

"As ready as I'll ever be. I might be more nervous than you."

"I wish I could reassure you, but I'm pretty fucking nervous."

"Well, we've got this." I grabbed my evening bag and let the door shut behind me.

Nash crooked his elbow and I slid my hand through it as we walked toward the elevators.

"Are any of your friends or teammates coming?" I asked him.

He shook his head. "No. Normally, I would have invited Lars and Sheridan and Wes and Hadley, but I don't need an audience for what may go down tonight."

"My only question at this point is, do we drink to relax or stay sober in case things go sideways?"

"I'm definitely having one," he said. "Beyond that, I have no idea."

"Okay."

We were quiet the rest of the way down the elevator and through the lobby to the ballroom where the party was taking place. Obviously, his father had spared no expense for the event, and that made no sense to me. Why make such a big deal out of something that no longer existed? They were still married, but he'd been having an affair for years.

"Nash!" A woman's voice broke through my reverie and I turned to see a middle-aged woman with Nash's eyes coming toward us, arms outstretched.

"Mom." Nash moved away from me and caught her up in a huge hug, holding her tightly.

"I've missed you so much," she said, tears filling her eyes.

"I know. I'm sorry. I'll do better this summer."

"Okay." She blinked away her tears and turned to me, curiosity mingling with the smile on her face. "Hello. I'm Nita Reilly, Nash's mother."

"It's so nice to meet you." I smiled back. "I'm Sariah Ansari."

She took my hand, giving Nash the side-eye. "I didn't realize Nash was seeing someone—and I must say, you are absolutely stunning, Sariah. Your dress is incredible."

"Th-thank you." Somehow, I couldn't find the words to correct her assumption about Nash and me.

"Mom, Sariah and I are—"

"Nash!" A deep, booming voice made me start and I turned to see a man who had to be Nash's father striding toward us, hand outstretched. "So good to see you, son!"

Nash sidestepped a hug, shaking his hand instead. "Dad."

"Carl, meet Nash's girlfriend Sariah. Isn't she lovely?" Nita looked pleased as punch and I was torn between correcting her and just leaving it alone. It felt like such a small thing in the grand scheme of shit that could potentially blow up tonight.

"Hello! Nice to meet you! Carl Reilly!" Everything he said and did was loud and over the top, and there was no doubt where Nash got some of his gregarious personality. The difference, of course, was that Nash knew when to tone it down and his father obviously hadn't figured that out yet.

"Nash, there are so many people here that want to see you," Nita said. "And your grandmother is at the table already. You know she doesn't move around so well anymore."

"Of course. I can't wait to see her." Nash sent a disgruntled look in his father's direction before reaching for my hand and tugging me forward.

"Nash!" A tall, beautifully coiffed blond in a slinky black dress and a bright smile ran in our direction.

I mentally groaned but Nash turned his face before she could kiss him and immediately pulled me against his side. "Hey, Jana. Good to see you."

She looked me up and down appraisingly before deciding I wasn't worth the time and turned back to Nash.

"Sariah, this is my cousin's wife, Jana. Jana, this is Sariah."

"I didn't realize you were dating anyone." She looked almost offended, and I had to bite back a laugh.

This was obviously going to be a thing tonight, and every time we tried to correct the assumption, Nash's name was called out. He was pulled in a dozen different directions, and I made the subconscious decision to just let it go. This was already a clusterfuck. If I decided not to forgive Nash, I'd never see these people again and he could just tell his mom it didn't work out. He didn't need any other aggravation.

"I'm sorry," Nash breathed in my ear. "I'll set my mom straight about our relationship as soon as I get a second alone with her."

"Don't worry about it." I met his eyes. "Let's just get through tonight."

"Are you sure?"

"Yes." I nodded. "But don't push it with the public displays of affection."

A glint of mischief danced in his eyes, and I was so glad to see a hint of normal, playful Nash, I let him get away with it.

"Whatever you were just thinking, forget about it."

"So I can't even *think* about naughty stuff?" he asked, making a face. "That's not fair."

"Nope. No thinking, and minimal touching." I tried to be stern but couldn't quite pull it off.

"You can't stop me from thinking about what's

under that dress," he whispered in my ear, making goose bumps break out on my flesh.

"Nash..." I was second-guessing my decision to give him some leeway on this when his face turned from playful to furious. His eyes turned almost black and his grip on my arm became painful.

"Nash, what is it?" I turned, following his furious gaze.

"He fucking invited her. The son of a bitch invited her."

"Who?"

"Sandy. His fucking *mistress*."

CHAPTER TWENTY-EIGHT

Nash

"This whole thing is fucked," I said, tugging on the knot on my tie.

"It's next-level assholery," Sariah said, giving me a sympathetic look.

The tie was so damn *hot,* it was suffocating me. The humidity here was no joke, even in the evening. I tugged and grumbled until I literally said fuck it and pulled the damn thing off.

"That was productive," Sariah said in a dry tone.

I shoved the tie in my pocket and ran a hand through my hair. We were outside getting some air, which I'd needed within five minutes of arriving. I was still in shock that he'd brought Sandy. Coming here had been a huge mistake.

"It's not even the party my mom wanted," I ranted. "She wanted to have something at home in their garden with twinkle lights and a harp player, not some bullshit at a hotel ballroom."

"Why didn't she put her foot down?"

I threw both arms in the air. "Who knows? And also, there's no chance I'm going to pose for photos with them for that photographer they hired. Is there a bar cart out here? I need a drink."

A smile was playing on Sariah's lips as she said, "I think what you need is to sit down. You're making yourself even more agitated and sweaty pacing back and forth like that."

I took her advice, shrugging off my jacket and sitting down on a wooden bench while rolling up my shirtsleeves. Sariah sat down next to me. I focused on breathing deeply, in and out, my frustration cooling as we listened to the laughter and conversation drifting out the open doors of a side entrance to the ballroom.

"So…" Sariah said. When she didn't continue, I looked at her.

"What were you going to say?"

"I'm not sure if it's what you want to hear."

"I don't care about that. Just say it."

Her eye makeup was darker than usual, and her cleavage in that dress was an eleven. She looked so damn sexy tonight, and it was hard not to think about taking her hand, getting the hell out of here, and going back to our hotel.

"You think we should go?" I asked, hoping we were on the same page.

"God, no. That's not what I was going to say." She lowered her brows, aggravated. "I think you need to man up and tell your mom the truth."

I balked at that. "Here? Now?"

"I mean, you should call her aside and make sure she can make a private exit, but yes. Did you see her in there? Dressed up so beautifully and holding on to his arm? Would she be doing that if she knew the truth?"

I looked away, the thought making me feel a little sick. "No."

"Nash."

Turning to her, I met her gaze, which was a mix of soft and steely.

"The last time you decided to withhold something important from someone you care about, how did that work out?"

I slumped against the back of the bench, knowing she was right.

"Am I like him?" I asked her. "He says he hasn't told her because he doesn't want to hurt her, and… fuck." I shook my head and buried my face in my hands.

"And it hits close to home because you said that about telling me that you were Rob."

"I'm sorry," I said, my voice mournful. "I'll be the first to admit I've run from the hard parts of relationships all my life. I hate that I did that to you."

Sariah kicked off her heels and gave a moan of satisfaction, settling back on the bench.

"You can't change what you don't acknowledge," she said.

"I acknowledge that hearing you moan like that made me a little hard." I waggled my brows at her.

"Don't deflect."

I scoffed, grinning at her. "Okay, ballbuster."

She reached over and took my hand. "You and I are going to walk back in there, pull your mom aside, and tell her what she deserves to know."

"You think she'd want to hear it with all these people here?"

Sariah nodded. "Not in front of them, of course, but if it were me, I'd be sick later knowing I posed for photos and listened to his bullshit toast and danced with him while all these people watched, and one of them is his mistress. It's disgusting."

"You're right."

She cringed and let go of my hand. "You're seriously sweaty."

"Tell me about it."

She slipped her shoes back on and stood. "We're going back in there and finding your mom immediately."

I nodded. Now that we'd decided to do this, I wanted to get it over with as soon as possible.

We walked back into the ballroom and my mom's face lit up when she saw us coming.

"Nash, where have you been? I have some friends I want to introduce you to."

She walked us over to a group of six couples, and my father was talking to one of the men.

"We finally get to meet your famous son," one of the women said, hugging me.

I said hello to everyone, shook hands, gave hugs, and talked hockey. Apparently my parents had hosted playoff-viewing parties at their house and this group of people had been there.

"Have you tried your mother's pucking amazing ribs?" one of the women asked me. "They are to die for."

I looked at my mom, amused. "Pucking amazing?"

She laughed and shrugged. "I like themes when

I'm hosting. And it's hard to get creative with so many playoff games."

My father put his arm around her, gazing at her like a man in love. "She made these homemade Ding Dongs that looked like pucks. Isn't that clever?"

"Oh!"

My mom held up a finger and I turned to see who was trying to get her attention. It was a woman with a camera.

"Be right there, Samantha!" she said.

Hooking one arm through my father's and another through mine, she said, "It's time to get some photos with my favorite two men."

Fuck. I shot a panicked look at Sariah, and she gave me a wide-eyed, just-fucking-do-it look.

My heart was pounding as I said, "Hey Mom, before we do that, can Sariah and I have a word with you?"

She looked confused. "Right now?"

"Right now."

My father intervened. "Surely it's nothing that can't wait until after the pictures."

"It can't wait," I insisted. "It needs to be now."

Her smile was like a knife to my chest. It hurt to know that I was the reason her life was about to implode.

"Honey, if you'd like Sariah to be in the photos,

that's absolutely fine," my mom said. "Since you haven't brought a woman home in years, I'm assuming it's serious with you two."

I swallowed hard. If only that was what I wanted to tell her.

"Mom, let's just step away for a little bit," I said. "It won't take long."

"Nash," my father said sternly. "We have a lot of guests and a schedule to keep."

Fuck him. He was worried I was about to expose him. This was so long overdue.

"If I want to talk to my mom privately for five minutes, I will," I said curtly.

I led my mom away, Sariah following.

"Nash, what's come over you?" my mom murmured. "It's not like you to talk to your father that way."

"Never mind that," I said. "You just need to trust me on this."

I turned to Sariah. "Where should we go?"

She furrowed her brow, looking puzzled. "The rental car? I'm not sure where else we can have complete privacy."

"What is going on here?" my mom asked, as I led her out of the ballroom and to the front entrance of the hotel. "I have a ballroom full of guests in there, Nash. Can't we just talk right here?"

I handed the valet my ticket.

"No, Mom, we can't."

"Are you engaged?" She looked hopefully between Sariah and me. "Oh my god, are you pregnant, Sariah? Please tell me you're pregnant. I want grandchildren so badly, but I never wanted to pressure Nash."

This was so fucking painful. My dad had been playing my mom for so long, and I could have stopped it at any time. Sariah was right—it was time to man up.

The valet pulled up with my rental car, and when he opened the passenger door, my mom gave me a bewildered look.

"I'm not leaving my own party."

"Mom, just get in the car."

"Where are we going? This is crazy and you won't even tell me what's going on."

Sariah laid a hand on my mom's forearm. "Nita, there's something you need to know, and we're just asking you for five minutes to talk to you privately."

"Something's wrong." My mom's eyes widened with worry. "What's wrong?"

"Please just get in the car," I pleaded.

She did, and Sariah made sure her dress was fully inside before the valet closed her door. I opened Sariah's door and passed the valet a tip.

As soon as I pulled away from the hotel, my mom turned to me, concern etched on her face.

"What's going on, Nash? Just tell me."

I gripped the steering wheel of the car, trying to find the right words, but I was at a loss. There were no right words to describe something so wrong.

"Mom," I started, clearing my throat. "I'm really sorry to have to tell you this, and I'm sorry for doing it tonight, but there's something you have to know."

"I'm listening," she said impatiently. "Out with it already. Please."

I met Sariah's gaze in the rearview mirror. She nodded.

"Dad's cheating on you, Mom."

She laughed. "That's absurd, Nash. At our age? We're past the point of one of us running around on the other."

I pulled into a random strip mall parking lot and backed into a space, putting the car in park. I turned in my seat and focused on my mom now that I wasn't driving anymore.

"He's been cheating on you for a while. I know because he asked me to get him tickets to a hockey game in New York and when I went to surprise him there, he was with her."

There was a pause. "With who?"

I shook my head. "Sandy. That's her name. I've

been telling him for two years now that if he didn't tell you, I would, but I never had the balls until tonight, and I'm sorry, Mom. I'm sorry about all of it."

She looked straight ahead, the color draining from her face.

"Sandy," she said softly. "The woman from his office."

I sighed heavily.

"You're completely sure?" she asked. "For two years?"

"At least. That's when I found out about it. It's why I don't come home anymore, because I hate him for what he's doing to you."

"Oh god." She opened the car door, bent over, and threw up right there in the parking lot.

Sariah exited the back seat of the car and went to my mom, staying away from the puke while pulling a cloth handkerchief from her handbag and passing it to my mom. Then she put a hand on her shoulder.

"Whatever you need, Nita, just tell us. We'll take you anywhere you want. You can come stay in one of our rooms at the hotel if you want."

My mom sat up, laughing without a trace of amusement. "Oh, we're going back to the party. But first I need some water."

Sariah's eyes locked with mine, neither of us

saying a word for a few seconds. When I snapped out of my shocked state, I reached for the bottle of water I'd put in the middle console at the airport.

"Here's some water, Mom."

She opened it and took a long drink.

"Okay, let's head back."

"Mom, I'm not sure—"

She gave me a stern look. "I love you, Nash, but we aren't debating this. Take me back right now."

Sariah got in the back seat and closed the car door. Silently, I put the car back in drive and headed back toward the hotel. I left my car with the valet and Sariah and I followed my mom back to the ballroom. It was clear from her expression that she was a woman on a mission.

"What the fuck is happening right now?" Sariah hissed at me. "I thought we'd go to a bar or something and get drunk with her."

"I don't know. This caught me off guard, too."

When my mom walked back into the ballroom, she was once again all smiles. As she made her way toward the stage, she stopped to say hello to someone.

"Portia, so good of you to come. How's Richard feeling?"

I stood near the back of the room with Sariah,

watching with a mix of horror and deep admiration as my mom made her way onto the stage and motioned for the string quartet to stop playing. As soon as they did, she took the microphone from its stand.

"Everyone, can I have your attention, please?"

The conversation quieted as everyone turned to look at my mom. Sariah took my hand. I was pretty sure we were both holding our breath.

"Thank you, everyone," my mom said, the picture of grace and composure. "I'd like to ask my husband Carl to come up on stage with me for a toast."

My gaze cut to my father, who was standing in a group with several other people, one of who was Sandy. Fucking asshole.

He smiled, set down his drink and made his way up on stage. When he got there, he kissed my mom on the cheek and put an arm around her.

"This is not what I imagined would be happening," Sariah whispered.

"Everyone, Carl and I can't thank you enough for coming tonight," my mom said. "We're celebrating thirty years of marriage."

The crowd clapped and the gentle clang of metal on glass sounded. My father moved to kiss my mother, but she spoke before he got there.

"Carl, can you tell all our friends and family how many of those years you've been cheating on me?"

The room went deadly silent. My father's eyes widened, but he said nothing.

"Oh." My mother smiled pleasantly. "Well, if you don't want to tell me, maybe your mistress will. Sandy, can you come up here, too?"

Gasps sounded, followed by a hushed murmur.

"Is Sandy still here?" my mom asked. "The blond from Carl's office?"

All eyes landed on Sandy, who ducked, letting her hair curtain her face as she ran from the room.

"Well," my mom said, still sounding like she was having the best time ever. "We won't be celebrating an anniversary tonight, but the caterers have already been paid for and there will be music until eleven. Please feel free to stay and enjoy yourself. The crepes are amazing. I did a lot of taste tests with the caterer to get them just right." She put the microphone back in its stand and leaned down to speak in it again. "Also, to the miserable, lying, piece of shit excuse for a man by my side, I'm divorcing you. Go to hell, Carl."

There was scattered applause as she left the stage. She smiled and strode back through the center of the room like a queen, stopping by Sariah and me.

"We can go now."

She started walking toward the door with Sariah and I following behind.

"I love your mom," Sariah murmured.

CHAPTER TWENTY-NINE

Sariah

IT WAS A LONG NIGHT. We took Nita home and I helped her pack a couple of suitcases while Nash got her a seat on our flight home to St. Louis in the morning. She would be going with us and staying with Nash for a few weeks while she cleared her head and the dust settled. She was heartbroken but still in the pissed-off phase, so there hadn't been much in the way of tears yet. Nash booked her a room at the Marriott by the airport so it would be easy to pick her up in the morning and then we bought her dinner and talked.

By the time we got back to our hotel, it was nearly one in the morning and Nash looked exhausted. I slid an arm around his waist as we rode up in the elevator, gently rubbing my palm up and down his torso in what I hoped was a soothing motion. He didn't react, other than to drop his chin to his chest, and my heart broke a little for him.

We walked as far as my door, since his was down the hall a little, and he finally looked at me. "Thank you. For tonight. I don't know if I could have gotten through this without you."

"I'm so proud of you," I whispered. "You did the right thing. For yourself and for your mom. I know it feels shitty now, but in the long run, she'll be better off."

"I know. It was just so fucking hard."

"But look at how she handled it. I mean, getting up there on that stage? Outing him in front of every-one? It was brutal and badass and cathartic. You get your strength from your mother. You know that, don't you?"

"I didn't," he said quietly. "But I guess I do now."

I waved my key over the lock and the little green light flashed, indicating I could open the door. I hesitated for a fraction of a second before looking up at him. "Do you want to come in?"

His eyes met mine with a silent question.

I couldn't answer him just yet, so I tugged his hand instead, pulling him inside.

He'd long since lost his jacket but the way he looked in his dress shirt, with several buttons open at the throat, made me want to lick a trail there. He was impossibly attractive, and after what we'd been through tonight, I wanted to lose myself in him. And allow him to lose himself in me. But there had to be a conversation first.

I kicked off my heels and then turned my back to him. "Can you unzip me?"

His eyes widened as he stepped forward. "Sariah, if this is some twisted way of teasing me…"

"Not tonight," I said quietly. "Not after what we just went through."

He nodded and I felt the zipper slide down.

"Do you want to touch me?"

I wasn't sure if I heard or felt his gasp of surprise, but then he shocked me by saying, "No. Not if this is a pity thing."

I let the dress drop to my hips and slowly turned. I wore nothing but thong panties and I slowly shimmied the rest of the way out of the dress.

"Shirt," I said in a firm voice.

"Sariah, what—"

"Shirt." I spoke louder, raising my hands to my breasts and slowly squeezing.

"Aw, fuck, Sariah."

"Do you want to work this thing out between us?"

I'd never seen anyone unbutton and discard a shirt faster than he did.

"Pants."

I had him remove the rest of his clothes, except his boxers, one piece at a time until we were standing there in our underwear. I'd seen him naked before, but this was different. Tonight would be different, depending on the direction the conversation we were about to have went.

"Almost from our first conversation," I said softly. "When you were Rob and I was the crazy woman with the dead cat, there was something special about you. You were kind. Gentle, considering the circumstances of those first texts. When I met you in person, on some level, I knew. Not consciously, of course. But Rob and Nash both had no trouble breaking down my emotional barriers, unlike anyone I'd ever known, no matter how hard I tried to stop it. I started to fall hard and fast. And then you hurt me."

His gaze dropped, a soft sigh escaping him. "I'm so sorry, babe."

"I know." I reached out and lifted his chin, forcing him to meet my gaze. "What do you want, Nash?"

"You."

"Specifically."

"Everything. I want you to be with me, live with me if you want to, have a relationship with the pups, stand by my side through the good and the bad. All of it. Whatever you want from me, I'm willing to give."

"Monogamy."

"Fuck yes." His blue eyes flashed liquid sapphire. "There hasn't been another woman since the first text, Sariah. In the very beginning, it wasn't intentional, I won't lie about that—it just didn't happen. But within a week or two of conversation, I couldn't think of anyone else."

"We'd have to have a conversation with the powers that be with the Mavericks. I know there isn't a rule about dating, but I don't think anyone from the front office has ever dated a player. I won't give up my job."

"I wouldn't expect you to and I'll make sure it's okay on every level."

I took a breath. This was my last question and it was a big one. The biggest one. The one that would make or break us. Especially me.

"Do you love me, Nash?"

His whole demeanor changed. He softened. His face, his body language, everything about him turned into someone I didn't recognize for a moment. Until his eyes sought out mine and he ever so gently reached for me, drawing me closer. Looking into my eyes, with only a couple of inches between us, he whispered, "I fucking adore you. I've never been in love before, not as an adult, and you fill something in my soul that I never even realized was empty. I love you so fucking much, Sariah."

Tears puddled in my eyes as his lips found mine. But instead of devouring me the way I'd hoped, he kept it simple. Light. His lips hovering, caressing, teasing.

"I have two questions," he whispered against my mouth.

"Hmm?" My eyes fluttered open.

"Why did we do this in our undies?"

"Because even the most laid-back, unemotional guy is more vulnerable like this. I know I am. And we've already slept together, so it wasn't about seeing each other naked."

"Ah." He reached out and brushed my hair back so it cascaded down my back while his eyes drifted lower and lower.

"And your second question?" I asked after a moment.

His gaze lifted back to mine, his face as sincere as I'd ever seen it. "Do you love me?"

I'd known it was coming but saying it out loud

made me more vulnerable than I'd ever been because I knew with everything in my heart, Nash had the power to destroy me. Theo had hurt me; I would never recover if Nash betrayed me again.

"So much." A tear slipped down my cheek and he brushed it away with his fingers.

"Can't you say the words?"

"They scare me. *You* scare me. If you change your mind…"

"Never gonna happen." He pulled me up against him, his warm hands caressing my lower back. "I swear to you, Sariah. I will never hurt you. Not as long as I'm alive."

"Kiss me, Nash."

"Tell me you love me, babe."

I couldn't breathe as I stared up at him. My heart jumped in staccato beats against my chest as I licked my lips, mustering up the courage to bare my soul to this beautiful man. He'd hurt me, but I knew now that it was a mistake, a temporary lapse in judgment during a stressful situation. A man who loved dogs, took care of his mom, and got teary-eyed at his teammate's wife's funeral wasn't a man who would intentionally hurt me. Not again.

Never again.

"I…" I swallowed. "Will you say it first…again? Please?"

He smiled. "I love you, baby."

"I love you too."

This time he crashed his mouth to mine, kissing me like a man starved. Our bodies molded together, my breasts flattened against his hard chest, his hands squeezing my ass as his tongue pillaged mine. He sucked and licked and kissed me until my knees started to buckle. Then he scooped me up and carried me to the bed, dropping me with a soft thud.

"Panties off," he whispered in a husky voice, shucking his boxers. He stood at the foot of the bed stark naked, his erection jutting up thick and proud, waiting for me to comply. I quickly tugged my thong off and started to toss it but he grabbed it midair.

"Mine," he said, with a predatory smile that made my insides clench with arousal.

He took a moment to put it in the pocket of his discarded dress pants before coming back to crawl onto the bed.

"Do you trust me, Sariah?"

"I just gave you the most important thing I have," I whispered. "Do you need to ask?"

"I do. Because I don't have a condom with me."

Our eyes locked and understanding dawned.

"Yes." This time, I didn't hesitate. "I'm on the pill and I do trust you."

His eyes danced with raw lust. "Spread those beautiful thighs for me. Let me see how wet you are."

I let my legs fall open but instead of kneeling between them, he crawled up my body and his lips sought mine. He kissed me thoroughly, his lips and tongue devouring mine—hell, he was devouring me —in the best way possible. His big hands were tendrils of pleasure everywhere he touched me and I groaned when his lips traveled down to my breasts. He cupped one in his hand, flicking his tongue over my already erect nipple. He teased and sucked until my chest arched up, demanding more.

He chuckled, moving to the other breast and giving it the same attention, driving me wild.

"Fuck, you're beautiful when you're turned on."

I whimpered when he used one thick finger to slide through my folds. I hadn't realized how aroused I was until now. I felt my wetness as he teased me, sliding up and down, touching everything but my clit. He slid down my body, peppering soft, feathery caresses on my skin until finally—*finally*— he was between my legs. He leaned forward and softly kissed my mound, hands pushing my thighs even farther apart.

"Nash…" I moaned with need. "Please."

His mouth was sinfully perfect, doing things that made my hips shoot up off the bed and crazy groans escape my chest. He pressed a finger inside of me as he sucked my clit between his lips and I shrieked, so close to orgasm, but he pulled back.

"Not yet." He pushed his tongue inside of me and I started to pant, my hips canting toward his mouth, desperate for the release he continued to deny me.

"Nash…" My voice sounded whiny, desperate, and he laughed softly, teasingly.

"Say it," he growled. "Tell me what you want."

"You. Inside me."

"Uh-uh. Say the dirty words, baby."

"Fuck me, Nash. Take that thick, hard cock of yours and fuck me like you mean it."

To my astonishment, he lifted to his knees in the blink of an eye and thrust all the way in with one hard push.

"Holy…" My eyes might have rolled back in my head, I wasn't sure, but words failed me as he started to move.

This wasn't tender or romantic; he was doing exactly what I'd asked.

Every glide out made me whimper and every tilt of his hips made me gasp with pleasure. He grabbed both of my hands in one of his, holding them over my head as he thrust in and out of me. There was something animalistic about the way he was taking me, and I gave myself over, letting him control everything. Me, my pleasure, us.

"More?" he growled against my mouth.

"Yes. Fuck yes!"

Every subsequent thrust hit a spot inside of me that made my back arch up off the bed, and he used his free hand to grasp the back of my neck.

"I'm so fucking close," he whispered. "Come when I do, baby."

"Yes, yes, yes!" He didn't have to ask because I was already on the edge. His words pushed me over and I screamed my release, bucking and writhing as he spilled himself inside of me.

"Fuck, that was beautiful." He collapsed on top of me, pressing light kisses along my jaw.

"Holy shit." My eyes were still closed as I tried to come back to earth because whatever that was had been otherworldly.

"God, I missed you." He slowly pulled out and rolled onto his back, pulling me into his arms.

"Me too." I nestled deeper into him, still trying to catch my breath.

We were quiet for a few minutes before I managed to find my voice. "Say it again, Nash."

His arms tightened around me because he knew exactly what I meant.

"I love you, beautiful."

CHAPTER THIRTY

Nash

"YOU SURE ABOUT THIS?" Alvarado asked me as we stepped out of my car in front of Sawyer's house.

"A little late to be asking that, don't you think?" I said, putting my car keys in my pocket.

"I just meant that I could stay in the car." He gestured back at my car with his thumb. "I haven't been on the team very long and he might not want me in his house."

In a group text with everyone on the team except Sawyer, we were making sure someone from the team checked in on him at least every other day. He was taking Annie's death hard, and we wanted him to know we were all there for him. Even our most annoying rookie.

"This is part of being on our team," I told Alvarado. "The team is a family. You're like the youngest kid in the family. The one who just hit puberty and jerks off in his bedroom all the time."

He rolled his eyes. "When are you going to stop busting my balls?"

I laughed and shook my head. "When it stops being fun. Which won't be anytime soon."

I rang Sawyer's doorbell. It took him a couple minutes to answer it, and when he did, I pressed my lips together to avoid him seeing my surprise.

Dude looked like absolute shit—even worse than when I'd seen him last week. He hadn't shaved since Annie died more than two weeks ago, and he'd gone from clean-shaven to sporting a short, dark beard. His hair was going in a hundred different directions and he was wearing the same Mavericks T-shirt and pajamas he'd had on last week; I just didn't know if he'd washed them since then.

"What's up?" he said, looking like we'd woken him up even though it was two in the afternoon.

"Just coming by to see how you are," I said.

"I'm fine."

I scowled. "Well, we drove all the way over here so at least invite us in for a beer, asshole."

He stepped aside. "Yeah, come on in. The place is a mess."

There was a blanket on the couch and at least a dozen empty beer cans on the coffee table. Alvarado and I exchanged a look as we sat down.

"I'll get us some beers," Sawyer said.

"No, forget the beers," I said.

"I don't mind. I've got plenty."

It was obvious he was drinking a lot, and I didn't want to add more fuel to that fire.

"It's fine. Just sit down and come talk to us," I said. "Have you left the house since the last time I was here?"

He rolled his eyes. "Why does it matter to you?"

"I don't want you sitting here feeling like shit all day every day, man."

"I watched my wife die. How else do you expect me to feel?"

I sighed heavily, looking to Alvarado for help.

"Is this what Annie would want for you?" he asked.

Sawyer's expression darkened. "She's gone, dipshit. And trust me, you have no idea what it's like to experience a loss like this."

"You're right, I don't. It's…" His voice trailed off and he didn't finish.

"What?" Sawyer demanded. "What is it?"

"Never mind," Alvarado said.

"No, tell me. Seriously."

Alvarado exhaled, ran a hand through his hair, and scooted to the edge of the recliner he was sitting in.

"It's different than losing your wife in other ways. Which is what just happened to me."

I gave him a puzzled look. "What do you mean?"

"My wife left me. She said she met someone else, and that someone else is the contractor remodeling our house. They were fucking, in our goddamn bed, while I was on the road. And the worst part is that I'm stuck with the house now. What am I supposed to do with a house my wife's lover renovated?"

"Sell it," Sawyer said.

"Yeah, I'll probably have to. In the meantime, I'm sleeping on the floor in one of our guest rooms because the remodel is now done, but we hadn't moved any furniture back in, and now she's moving in with him."

"What the fuck?" I asked, completely shocked.

I'd always assumed Alvarado and his pastor's-daughter wife were one of those couples that would do it missionary style three times a week, have two point five kids and retire to Florida, where they'd peacefully die within a few hours of each other once they got old.

"Sorry." Alvarado put a hand up. "I didn't mean to make things about me. I just wanted to show you that Annie might have passed, but she loved you with everything she had."

Sawyer shook his head. "Don't apologize, man. It's nice to have something else on my mind for a change."

"Are you guys getting divorced?" I asked.

Alvarado scoffed. "Yeah, of course. And there was no prenup, so that'll be a nice hard ass fucking."

Sawyer stood up. "I'm getting some beers."

He brought in three cold Bud Light cans, and we all cracked them open.

"Shit," I said.

"Yeah," Alvarado said. "Anybody got any good news?"

"Sariah's giving me another chance," I said.

"Good," Sawyer said. "She seems like a nice girl. Don't fuck it up."

We drank our beers in silence for a few seconds, each lost in our own thoughts.

"What's the contractor's name?" I asked Alvarado.

"Shawn McCoy, why?"

"I've got a few bumper stickers that would look good on his work truck. There's an *I love crack whores*, *I love dick*, and *Honk if you have herpes*. Take your pick, man."

Sawyer busted out laughing. Alvarado followed, and soon all three of us were cracking up.

"Like that magnet shit you kept putting on my truck?" Alvarado asked.

"No, these are stickers. They'll be a bitch to get off. I ordered them when I was pissed at you about Sariah."

Alvarado burst out laughing again, and Sawyer's smile reached his eyes for the first time in a while.

I took out my phone and said, "Let's order pizza. You got plenty of beer in the fridge?"

"Yep," Sawyer said. "Nothing in there but pickles and beer. We're good."

These two were both going through some shit, but at least they knew they weren't going through it alone.

—————

"Oh god, poor Eric," Sariah said later that evening when we were lying on my couch together.

"Yeah, I can't imagine."

"Hopefully he can get the divorce worked out during the off-season."

"You got any cute friends who like dipshit rookie hockey players?" I asked.

"I'm pretty sure Eric's not going to be up for dating for a while."

"Yeah, I guess not."

She sat up and crossed her legs, her eyes meeting mine.

"I was thinking pizza for dinner. Does that sound good?"

After eating a shitload of pizza at Sawyer's house only a few hours ago, it didn't sound remotely good, but I didn't want to disappoint her.

"Sounds great, babe. I can order from Davinci's because they'll deliver and they know how to make each of the dogs a little personal pizza, too."

She laughed and looked over at Athena, Louie, and Archie, who were lying on the floor right next to the couch.

"The dogs get their own pizzas?"

I feigned indignation. "Of course they do. What kind of barbarian dog dad do you think I am?"

"Can we watch a rom-com?" she asked.

Ugh. That sounded even worse than more pizza.

"How about if I let you pick what kind of pizza we get, and you can choose whether we watch porn or a horror movie?"

"Porn?" She arched her brows, looking amused. "Are you serious?"

"I mean…I'm a dude, so I'm not *not* serious. But horror is good, too."

"Hmm. Can we find a rom-com with some horror in it?"

"I doubt it?"

She considered how she'd up the ante. "Rom-com, and I'll take my bra off and let you feel me up through the entire movie."

"Done."

Joke was on her. If I had unfettered access to her tits, I'd have her in bed within half an hour and I'd never have to watch the rest of whatever movie she picked.

I ordered the pizzas while she scrolled through my Netflix menu looking for a movie to watch. Once she'd settled on one, I grabbed a blanket and we both got comfortable. She slid her hands up her back and unclasped her bra, sliding it out from beneath her shirt. I wasted no time occupying my hands.

"Did you talk to your mom today?" she murmured during the movie's opening credits.

"It's weird talking about my mom while I'm playing with your nipples."

"Just yes or no, Nash."

"No. She left me a message and said my aunt got into town to help her pack."

"Good."

My mom had stayed with me for a little while after the anniversary party from hell. Now she was back home packing up her things and selling some others, and moving to St. Louis. She was going to rent a place near me until she figured out where she wanted to be long term. I was hoping St. Louis would grow on her and she'd stay.

My father had agreed to an uncontested divorce in which my mom got half of their assets and all the furnishings in the house. It was the one decent thing he'd done for my mom. He hadn't made an effort to talk to me since the party, and I hoped he never would. I'd lost all respect for him, and I'd never spend time with him and Sandy.

"I should probably just take your shirt off to make this easier," I said.

"You think?"

"Yeah." I pushed up her shirt and put my lips around one of her taut pink nipples.

"Oh," she moaned. "We're not even five minutes into the movie and you're already trying to get me to ditch it."

"Me? No, I'm super into this movie."

I tweaked one nipple and gave the other a gentle nip.

Sariah laughed, then ran a hand through my hair

and grabbed it, tugging hard enough to get my attention.

"If we pause this movie for sex, we're still watching it afterward," she said.

"Wow." I slid a hand around to her ass and cupped it. "I'm just sitting here enjoying this movie and you're suggesting we pause it to go have sex?"

"I mean, if you don't want to…"

I gave her a quick kiss on the lips and smiled. "I definitely do."

I kissed her again, deeper this time, and she cupped my cheeks, her lips smiling against mine.

"I hope you're always this turned on by me when I'm wearing leggings and an old T-shirt with no makeup."

I grinned. "Believe me, I will be. Especially if you keep wearing my T-shirts."

Her eyes softened. "Nash Reilly, don't let this go to your already inflated head, but I think you might be my favorite."

"Yeah? Your favorite what, babe?"

"Everything."

I would have done anything she asked in that moment. Sariah was quickly becoming my best friend, and when she said things like that—things that told me how much I meant to her—it reinforced what a great idea falling in love with her was. I wasn't falling alone. We were in this together, now and always.

"Bet I can make you come twice before the pizza gets here," I said.

She arched a brow. "Probably. But then we're finishing this movie."

I put my hands up in mock surrender. "Yeah, I was really into it until you said I have to go fuck you."

She scoffed, her eyes dancing playfully. "Okay, big talker, you've got like twenty-five minutes to give me two orgasms. Ticktock."

She tried to leap over the back of the couch, but I caught her and pulled her back onto it, catching most of her weight on me. Her yelp was interrupted by her laughter.

"I'd better get to work right here on the couch then," I said.

As I tugged her pants down, she moaned her approval.

And in just seventeen minutes, I held up my end of our bargain.

EPILOGUE

Sariah

FOR THE FIRST time since I was a teenager, summer vacation was awesome. Though I still worked part-time, the fact of the matter was that I didn't have to work that hard. I had clients, a good salary, and the executive offices were essentially a ghost town in the summer. Everyone took time off and I even got two weeks of paid vacation, which I hadn't been expecting this soon after being hired. Lance said they didn't worry about accrual or anything like that. Rosa's strategy was that happy employees made the best employees, and she was probably right. So Nash and I jetted off to Antigua, and then I'd put in some hours while he'd gone to Asheville to help his mom close on her house.

Now it was late August and Nash had asked me to move in. I'd resisted because of my lease and everything, but then he'd come up with what I had to admit was a brilliant idea. His mom moved into my apartment and would stay there for the remainder of my lease, which would give her time to decide when and where she wanted to settle, and I moved in with Nash.

This created the only hiccup in our relationship —my family. My sisters knew I was dating someone but I'd been super careful not to tell them who. We'd come a long way since the old country, but bringing my all-American blond, blue-eyed boyfriend home to my Middle Eastern family was terrifying. It wasn't that they expected me to marry someone from Iran, but our disparate backgrounds might be tricky. Theo, at least, had been Italian and his family had been as old school as mine, just in a different way.

"It's going to be fine," Nash said for the hundredth time as we pulled up to my parents' house.

"How many girlfriends have introduced you to their parents?" I demanded, nervously wiping my hands on my denim miniskirt.

He got out of the car and came around to open my door for me. "As an adult?"

"Exactly."

"Babe." He reached for me and pulled me close. "I love you and they're going to see that I have the best of intentions."

I gently reached up to put my hand on the side of his face. "I know. It's just—" I faltered as a very familiar car pulled into the driveway. "Nash…what is your mother doing here?"

"What?" He swung around, frowning, and then walked over to where his mother was getting out of her car.

"Hello, sweetheart." She leaned up and kissed his cheek. "Will you get the casserole out of the passenger side? Hi, Sariah!"

"What are you doing here, Mom?" Nash asked, frowning.

"Nita!" A woman I assumed was Sariah's mother came out of the front door smiling. "You're late."

"I know." Nita gave her a little shrug. "I lost track of time."

"Well, come in, come in." She turned to Nash. "Hello. You must be Nash. I am Sadie Ansari, Sariah's mother."

"H-hello." Nash seemed nervous as he shook my

mother's hand, which wasn't like him at all, and I rushed forward.

"Mom." I quickly hugged her.

"You look beautiful," she said, smiling. "Like a woman in love."

I might have blushed.

"Hello, hello!" My father came to the door and the introductions started.

This wasn't at all what I'd envisioned.

"Does anyone want to tell us how you know Nash's mother?" I asked when everyone had finally been introduced.

"I hadn't seen you all summer," Mom said, lifting her chin a notch. "I suspected you and your mysterious new boyfriend were getting serious, and I figured the only way I was going to meet him would be to show up at your apartment unannounced. Imagine my surprise when a strange woman answered the door."

"But it's all straightened out now," Nita said, grinning. "And we decided to surprise you today."

Nash gave his mother a look. "You never used to be devious."

"Well, it was about time." She smiled.

"You cannot get married before me," Sami announced, frowning at me. "We're already in the planning stages and—"

"Stop." I held up a hand. "We're nowhere near the marriage stage. We just moved in together. We need time to adjust to being a couple."

"Not me." Nash shook his head solemnly. "I'm ready when you are."

My mouth fell open until I saw the laughter bubbling beneath the surface. "Nash…"

"I like him," my father stage-whispered to me.

We all laughed and conversation moved to the upcoming hockey season. My father, Felipe, and Sebastian seemed to be fully invested in the Mavericks, and I was happy to let them talk. I went into the kitchen to help with dinner and my sisters immediately pounced.

"He's dreamy," Sophia said. "Oh my god, he definitely doesn't need Photoshop."

I chuckled. "He does not."

"You are going to make the most gorgeous babies," Mom said, fanning herself. "Please tell me you want children."

"Eventually," I said firmly. "But give us time, okay? I don't want to rush this. He's too important."

"I know." She squeezed my arm. "I can see how important he is by the way you look at him—and by the way he looks at you."

"Theo never looked at you like that," Sami whispered, smiling.

"I know." I swallowed, suddenly emotional. "I had no idea there was someone like him out there for me. I didn't…" I broke off, swiping at my eyes. "I really thought I'd settle."

"Oh, my sweet girl." Nita looked horrified. "Don't do that. Even if by some crazy twist of fate you don't wind up with Nash, please don't ever settle."

"I won't," I said. "I *can't*. Now that I've felt love like the love Nash and I have, I could never settle for less."

———

DINNER WAS LOUD AND BOISTEROUS, with laughter and good food and too much wine. After we cleaned up, my dad and Felipe fell asleep watching baseball, Sophia went to take care of Reva, and my mother and Nita retired to the kitchen. Sami and Sebastian disappeared somewhere, and I wound up in a recliner on Nash's lap.

"I think today went well," he whispered in my ear, one hand softly stroking my knee.

"I think so too." I leaned into him, resting my head on his chest. "Our mothers are forces to be reckoned with, though."

"I know." He chuckled. "It's terrifying."

"They're going to be pushing us for marriage and babies on a regular basis."

"That's okay." He kissed the top of my head. "They can push all they want. You and I will figure all that out when the time is right for us. No one else."

"You make me so happy, Nash."

"Right back atcha, babe."

"Do you think hockey season is going to be hard on us?"

"In what way?"

"We didn't really get together until the season was over, so this is going to be new territory. You traveling, me navigating sales calls from people who will inevitably know we're dating, people I work with potentially having shit to say about it."

"I've already spoken to Lance and Rosa," he said. "There is no issue with us dating. Lance's biggest fear is that you're going to quit to be a stay-at-home wife and mom. Apparently, you outsold the rest of the entire sales team put together between March and the end of the season."

I chuckled. "Well, I guess that'll give them something else to rib me about. And when the time comes for babies, we might have to discuss me staying home, but not anytime soon."

"Agreed."

"Everett wants us to come to dinner."

"I'd like that."

There didn't seem to be anything else to say and I may have dozed off as Nash watched the baseball game.

"Hey, wake up, sleepyhead." Nash gently nudged me awake and I sat up, looking around.

"Oh, shit, how long did I sleep?"

"About an hour, but everyone's getting ready to go."

"Oh." I sat up and we said our goodbyes before heading home.

Home.

Nash's house was now my house too and while I'd been a little uncomfortable about it in the beginning, now that I'd settled in, it felt good.

The truth was that everything with Nash felt good. I was a tiny bit nervous about the season starting and everyone at the office seeing that I was with Nash, but mostly I didn't care. My work spoke for itself, and I felt strongly that our love would carry us through. There would inevitably be tough times, but we'd get through them together.

"I'm tired," I murmured. "I think I had too much wine."

"I'm happy to take you to bed. Go relax and I'll be right in after I take the dogs out."

"Okay." I headed toward our bedroom and went into the bathroom. I took off my makeup, washed my face, and brushed my teeth. Then I stripped and got into bed. We always slept naked. Not because he expected it but because his touch had become addictive. I loved the feel of his big hands on my skin, and it had nothing to do with sex. The sex was great too, obviously, but his touch was something else.

I must have dozed off again because I started when he slid into bed behind me. His lips were soft on my shoulder.

"Go back to sleep, baby."

"I love you, Nash. Thank you for being you."

Those wonderful hands of his stroked their way down my sides. "Thank you for loving me. I'm finally the man I always hoped I'd be."

ABOUT THE AUTHOR

Brenda Rothert lives in Central Illinois with her husband, children and three dogs. She loves to hear from readers through her website or her Facebook Group, Rothert's Readers.

ABOUT THE AUTHOR

USA Today Bestselling author Kat Mizera was born in Miami Beach with a healthy dose of wanderlust. She's lived from coast to coast, and everywhere in between, but home is wherever her family is.

A devoted mom and wife to her wonderful and supportive husband (Kevin) and two amazing boys (Nick and Max), Kat loves to travel the globe with her adventurous, hockey loving family. Greece is at the top of that list. She hopes to one day retire there, spending her days writing books on the beach.

Kat is former freelance sports writer who now writes steamy hockey romance about her favorite fictional teams, the Las Vegas Sidewinders and the Alaska Blizzard. The library of novels she's penned also include sexy contemporary stories about baseball stars, alpha sex club owners, special forces heroes, rock stars and royalty. Regardless of genre, her books about bad boys with hearts of gold will steal your breath, rock your world and melt your heart.

WHERE TO FOLLOW KAT:

WEBSITE
FACEBOOK
TWITTER
INSTAGRAM
BOOKBUB
KAT'S PRIVATE FACEBOOK GROUP

ALSO BY BRENDA ROTHERT

CHICAGO BLAZE SERIES

Book 1 - Anton

Book 2 - Luca

Book 3 - Victor

Book 4 - Knox

Book 5 - Alexei

Book 6 - Easy

Book 7 - Jonah

Book 8 - Kit

Book 9 - Olivier

SIN CITY SAINTS SERIES

Book 1 - Maverick

Book 2 - Pike

ST. LOUS MAVERICKS SERIES

Book 1 - Hard Fall

Book 2 - Hard Limit

FIRE ON ICE SERIES

Book 1 - Bound

Book 2 - Captive

Book 3 - Edge

Book 4 - Drive

Book 5 - Release

His

Alpha Mail

Healing Touch

Barely Breathing

Anton

Alaska Blizzard:

Defending Dani

Holding Hailey

Winning Whitney

Losing Laurel

Saving Sara

Chasing Charli

A Very Blizzard Christmas

Tending Tara

Calling Cassie

Playing Peyton

St. Louis Mavericks (with Brenda Rothert)

Hard Fall

Hard Limit

Lauderdale Knights:

Slap Shot

Big Shot

Rock Hard:

Play

Pause

Rewind

Fast Forward

The Royal Trilogy:

Nowhere Left to Fall

Nowhere Left to Run

Nowhere Left to Hide

Royal Protectors:

Sandor

Cocky Protector (book 1.5, part of the Cocky Heroes
Club series)

Xander

Axel

Dax (*A Royal Protectors/Sidewinders crossover novel*)

Inferno:

Salvation's Inferno

Temptation's Inferno

Redemption's Inferno

Tropical Inferno (formerly "Tropical Ice")

Romancing Europe:

Adonis in Athens

Smitten in Santorini

Lucky in Lugano

Other Books:

Special Forces: Operation Alpha: Protecting Bobbi (Susan Stoker's Special Forces World)

Special Forces: Operation Alpha: Protecting Delilah (Susan Stoker's Special Forces World)

View Kat's entire collection of books at www.KatMizera.com